Winter Hunger

WINTER HUNGER

Cliff Schimmels

VICTOR BOOKS a division of SP Publications, Inc.
WHEATON. ILLINOIS 60187

Offices also in
Whitby. Ontario, Canada
Amersham-on-the-Hill, Bucks, England

Library of Congress Catalog Card Number: 85-50319
ISBN: 0-89693-333-4

VICTOR BOOKS
A division of SP Publications, Inc.
    Wheaton, Illinois 60187

Contents

CLIFF SCHIMMELS grew up near Wheatheart. He smelled the red earth, watched the wheat grow, ate at the local cafes, went to school with the Vince Benallis, and fell in love with the simplicity of rural life. After his schooling, he went back to a place near Wheatheart as a pastor and then as a teacher.

Since 1974, Dr. Schimmels has been Professor of Education at Wheaton College. He is the author of four books on education and the home, including *How To Help Your Child Survive and Thrive in the Public Schools* (Revell). He and his wife, Mary, have three children.

———————————

The smells and sounds of rural Oklahoma,
a sunset lingering in the west,
a cow grazing on the distant hill,
freshly plowed dirt, diesel smoke,
the growth and harvest of wheat—
it was all a part of my growing.
It is an inseparable part of me still.

To those people who taught me such things
as honesty, sincerity, loyalty, and the honor of work,
to those who opened their lives and invited me in,
I offer these Chronicles as a token of my gratitude.
I love you and cherish our times together
both in the present and in my remembering.

Cliff Schimmels
1985

"Meaningless! Meaningless!"
says the Teacher.
"Utterly meaningless!
Everything is meaningless!"

What does man gain
from all his labor
at which he toils
under the sun?

Ecclesiastes 1:2-3

1

The Want Lingers On
1980

Vince Benalli strolled around his kingdom. With his hands in his pockets and his head thrust back to indicate intent without purpose, he roamed the halls of Wheatheart High School, taking advantage of the quiet which falls over a school during the lazy time of the afternoon, when teachers drone on like late summer flies trapped against the windowpanes and students nap between notes.

Vince could stroll and roam as much as he liked, because he was the principal and was charged by the community to take care of the school and the 146 students entrusted to him. And that was what he was doing, taking care of his high school, earning his pay. He stopped and slammed shut a locker door left half open. "Freshmen!" he muttered. "They are so careless." He picked up scattered pieces of paper from where they had fallen when the students had scurried to classes after lunch. Some of the sheets looked as if they might have been important, like today's homework; but mostly they were high school stuff, notes between friends about boys and cheerleading practice, doodles drawn of airplanes fighting in midflight, or cowboys looking romantic with cigarettes hanging out of their mouths.

But it didn't matter to Vince what the papers were. They were still trash and he rolled them all into a tight ball. On his way to the wastebasket at the south end of the hall, he paused at the drinking fountain long enough to scrape up a piece of half-chewed purple bubble gum.

Moving on, he stopped at each classroom door and peered briefly through the little windows. He didn't have to look long. He was good enough at his job to see quickly and to record mentally. Joe Grimes was sitting still. That was unusual. Mrs. Hill was writing on the chalkboard. My, she's a good teacher . . . always prepared. Mary Beth and Kathleen Ann were passing notes. Well, at least they weren't talking. That Morris kid—Vince could never remember his first name, there were so many of them—had mud on his shoes. Where did he get mud on a day like this? Those Morrises were strange.

Having completed his survey, Vince went back to being in charge. He stood at the south door and looked down the hill and along Main Street—past the houses, past the Baptist Church, past the two blocks of stores and shops and the Dew Drop Inn Cafe, past the bank where his wife, Beth Ann, was president, past the drugstore with the doctor's office above. He looked all the way down Main Street to where it ended or began, depending on your position, at the John Deere store where the horizon was flecked with the green and yellow of farm implements sitting in the yard, waiting to be sold to the neighboring wheat farmers who were noted for producing grain and kids.

As he looked, Vince read the town, his town. Oh, he didn't know it as well as he knew the kingdom of his high school, but he knew it well enough to read it. He knew the pickup trucks parked along the street well enough to know who was gossiping where and which farmers were in town for business or break. He knew the town well enough to distinguish Doc's big dog, Spencer, dozing on the sidewalk outside the drugstore. He knew the town well enough to recognize the widows—farm wives, mostly, who moved to town when their husbands died—going home with small sacks of groceries. He knew the town well enough to look for the green and white banner hanging at the intersection, which commanded, WIN STATE, WHIPPETS. He knew it all; and that should have pleased him. But maybe he knew it too well. . . .

"I'm warning you. There ain't no place to hide in this town."

Those were angry words, shriller than the north November wind which gusted early across the barren fields, gathering baby wheat plants and red clay pebbles and pelting them against the double glass doors which separated the high school from that other world.

The retort was less shrill but more threatening. "I don't need to hide, Hot Dog! I'm not afraid of your big mouth and I'm not ashamed of the way I feel."

"You'd better be. Your feelings may get you a punch in the nose."

"Well, when you feel lucky, you'd better start punching, 'cause the way I feel is all I got. I can't change that."

Although eighty feet of hallway and a blind corner around the auditorium separated Vince Benalli from the origin of those sounds, he knew exactly what was going on. He hadn't been in that school twenty-three years for nothing. He knew his school and he knew his students, all 146 of them. Even now, he knew the scene, the combatants, and the cause. He had been down this road before, too many times for a day like this when the wind blew winter too soon, and the body and the soul felt the years they hadn't even lived yet.

The combatants were two football players—a starting halfback more important by position than he really was, and a second team lineman. The lineman, straining against the tablet of laws published by tradition, had been seen with the back's girlfriend. And this couldn't be tolerated in Wheatheart. The social code did not permit it, not even if the back was through with the girl or had mistreated her. Starting backs don't lose their girlfriends, not during the season and particularly during a season when a team is about to win the state championship. And backs never lose girls to linemen.

The lineman should have known that, but maybe he was inspired by whatever success comes to a second-stringer. Now the star had to teach that youngster a lesson. The code demanded it. He would shout him down in a public place, like the vacant hall during fifth period. The lineman, in order to save face and to speak for linemen everywhere, would shout back. If the shouting got loud enough and insulting enough, and maybe even filthy enough, perhaps someone would hear it and rush out before the warriors were forced to take the code a step further. But if no one interfered, there would have to be some pushing and shoving and grabbing. And if this ritual was performed with enough noise and delay, surely someone would come to the scene and pull those two struggling young animals apart before things really got out of hand. But if not, one of them would have to punch the other, just to prove that the code was still in force. The combatants really didn't want it to go that far. They wanted someone to arrive on the scene and step in. But they were bound by the code.

Vince knew all this. He could see it all so clearly, but he also knew the aftermath. Regardless of what happened, even before the end of the school day, the whole town would know about a terrible fight between two football players, "on the week of the state championship game, even!"

"What is happening to our school?"

"Where's the discipline?"

"Why is that place out of control?"

"It ain't like it was in the good old days."

Wherever the Wheatheart brain trust met to oversee human affairs—the Dew Drop Inn Cafe, the John Deere store, the grocery store, or Doc Heimer's waiting room—the rumors and the solutions would run thick and deep. By five o'clock, the rumors would have stretched to the far corners of the community—blood would have been splattered in the hall and those precious young men would have only narrowly escaped requiring emergency treatment at the hospital.

Fortunately, Vince was in the hall, where good principals ought to be. With his has-been athletic legs spurred by a little adrenalin, he could get there while the war was still in the shouting stage. And when the fighters spotted him, they would try to tackle each other, but he would step in and keep them apart. Tempers would cool. The three would walk cautiously down the hall to the office, and then Vince would spend the next hour trying to get to the bottom of a story he already knew. Just another game, but it filled the time and satisfied the code.

That's how it should have played out. But after nine years as principal, Vince had acquired other habits and impulses. Just before he turned the corner to come face to face with the two shouters, he ceremonially checked the door which opened onto the stairs leading down behind the auditorium to the now secluded basement room which once housed the boiler, before the school went on natural gas a quarter of a century earlier. The door was unlocked. The knob gave in to his touch. That door shouldn't have been unlocked! That was dangerous. That door should never be unlocked. Who knows what might happen if students ever found out about such a room! We couldn't have that. Mr. Casteel had said so himself, and he ought to know, because he had been superintendent for nearly thirty years.

Vince checked again to make sure he was alone in the hall, and then quietly slipped through the unlocked door and down the steps to the basement room. With an ease trained by habit, he found the switch above the one incandescent light bulb hanging from the ceiling. It filled the small room with the dim glow of solitude and secrecy. From a discarded teacher's desk, he pulled out a dog-eared copy of James Joyce's *Portrait of an Artist as a Young Man*. As he sat back casually in a discarded teacher's chair, he drew miles and years of distance between himself and the wind and the war which raged upstairs.

Vince had been working on this book for a couple of weeks, snatching a few pages every time he had a chance or a need to get away from things outside. He had tried to read it once before when he was still in college. That old professor, the one with the full beard, the red beret, and a silk scarf in place of a tie, the one who rode a bicycle across campus, had actually assigned the book in some class—maybe Modern British Authors. Most people went straight to the library, whipped out the Cliff's Notes and saved all the time. Farm boys from rural towns of the red-dirt and short-grass country didn't get too excited about investing much of their time in reading books recommended by bicycle-riding professors. But Vince was different. He tried to read all the assignments. He too thought the professor was a little weird; but he wanted to know what, if anything, made the James Joyces and Platos and Dantes of the world stand out from the Wheatheart farm boys. He had to know that.

Vince didn't like the *Portrait* during his college days. He was too young then to understand youth. Now, after all these years of studying young people, he read with intensity punctuated with hearty bolts of laughter and silent Amens, like a first-time father bending over his newborn baby. Or, maybe he was enjoying it simply because he was probably the only person in Wheatheart who had ever heard of the book, much less read it, and that thought pleased him!

But today he found himself impatiently fighting the words. At first, he blamed it on the flow, the choppy style, the stream of consciousness. But it wasn't that. And it wasn't the weather or the war. Vince was restless. He was plain restless in a contemplative way. On this day, he didn't like kids, didn't want to be around them. He didn't want to read about them. It wasn't their childish pranks or even the scuffles in the hall. Vince rather enjoyed childish behavior. Why else would he have chosen to stay on as teacher and principal, if he wasn't at least amused? No, there was something else that went much deeper. On this day, with winter threatening outside, Vince resented kids because of their dreams. Joyce's book was filled with dreams. Those 146 people upstairs were filled with dreams. They weren't living life now. They were just passing through to higher things. Passing through. In a weekend they could blow through more good times, more memorable events, than most people could expect to have in a decade. In a single good day at school, they could be exposed to more ideas and original thoughts and more opportunities than most people get in twenty years. And yet, they were just passing through. And Vince resented their smugness and their mobility.

Tossing the book back on the desk to a spot half hidden among more mundane papers and journals, Vince remembered that he was forty-six years old. Forty-six. There was nothing really magical about the number, not like the big celebrations that come with the turning of the decades when some practical joker puts an ad in the paper or a sign in your front yard. "Vince is forty!" "Vince is fifty!" That's different. Then, at least, someone is paying attention to you. Someone else is conscious of the passing of time too.

But when you are forty-six, nobody cares. There aren't any signs and celebrations. There you are, all alone, in the middle of middle age, and no one cares. The dreams are gone and no one cares. While the wind whistles outside, and while two young bulls push each other around in empty halls to prove a point of honor, your life and your dreams slip by unnoticed.

Forget the jokes. Forget the good-natured jibbing at the John Deere store or the cafe. Middle age is a reality. It used to be a whimsical time, like the opening line of a fairy tale, "Far away and long ago." But now it is nothing but cold reality.

As Vince leaned back in the chair with his feet propped up on the desk, he fixed his stare on some cobwebs and his attention on a search for the proper analogy for the way he felt. "Middle age is a harvest," he thought. Yes, that might be appropriate. It is a time when you reap all the decisions you have made through the years. At first, those decisions grow naturally and carelessly out of your dreams. The two go hand in hand. But somehow over the course of the years, those dreams get pushed aside, shoved away by the reality of decisions, until you find yourself forty-six and afraid to dream anymore. You are stuck, and you have no choice but to harvest what you have sown.

But there the analogy breaks down, at least in wheat country. Harvest is a time of excitement, activity, good feeling, warmth and sunshine and big meals. A time when you mix work and energy with thoughts of paying off your debts and starting all over again fresh.

But to Vince, middle-age harvest was anything but fresh. It was a time when days and events ran together, looking for a moment distinctive enough to hang a memory on. It was a time when he tried desperately to make the best of what he had, but never once allowed himself to dare to dream of planting a new crop. It was a time when he came to grips with the barren fact that this was all there was. No fanfares, no big meals and celebrations, no thoughts of the next harvest. Middle age was a time of the reality of decisions, and not the product of dreams. "Nope," Vince thought, "harvest is the wrong analogy." It implied that middle age would come barging in like a John Philip Sousa march. Instead, it had come like an Emily Dickinson poem, whimpering all the way.

Almost purposely, almost by habit, Vince rummaged in his pockets until he found a scrap of paper, yesterday's announcements folded four times, pertinent news once but now just more junk.

In the same pocket, he found a pen, a forty-nine cent Bic medium point, but it was red. "Oh, well," he grumbled aloud as if he and himself were on a joint adventure, "red will have to do. Maybe God likes red."

Writing in rapid spurts, with studied rests between, he plunged himself into the project at hand.

> Dear God, Father, Saviour, Healer,
> Who made the blind to see and the lame to walk,
> who brought order to the storm,
> who blew the waves and steadied the boat,
> who schooled the fish onto the right side,
> who sees and knows and takes charge—
> if I had pains I could feel,
> I would ask You to heal, and believe that You could.
> But what do I do with the pains I cannot feel?
> In faith I could trouble You
> with a broken leg or a broken heart,
> but not with the pain of a vacuum.
> My heart shrivels, and rattles around,

banging against the sides of my soul,
and the ache hurts worse than any pain.
Power? I am the principal!
Love? I am the husband!
Comfort? I live in ease enough to cause envy.
Yet, I don't want what is! I want what was
supposed to have been, but never can be!
I have what other men pray for, but it is all
squished down to the bottom of my being,
squashed by the weight of loneliness.
Heal me from the disease of having what I want—
all I want . . . and yet the want lingers on.
O Lord, please understand! Because no one else does.

Finished, Vince let the paper fall back into its four folds. It was too bulky that way to fit smoothly in his pocket, but since it was that way already, it was too late to change it.

When that attitude caught Vince's attention, he squinted hard as if to prevent a headache, leaned back and tried to remember why it was too late. His memory traced the years until it found an incident in the spring of 1957.

Trust Across the Chasm
1957

Nineteen hundred fifty-seven was a year that shocked the world. Scientists shot a ball into outer space, and that ball spun into an orbital pattern and circled the globe.

This was a giant step in human history. If a piece of iron could float around up there, maybe a man could. Think about that! A person could leave the earth's atmosphere. Maybe we would be walking on the moon someday.

And what was even worse, the Russians did it. Not the good old U.S.A. The Russians!

A panic, but a good panic, swept the nation and came blowing across the prairie. It was a good panic because it was competitive, the kind that said, "Let's roll up our sleeves and do something about this." A bad panic would have said, "Let's lie around and hope it goes away."

The year 1957 didn't find Vince Benalli lying around. For him, it was the year when goals turned to dreams and dreams turned to decisions and decisions took root and grew. He graduated from college. Since he was the first of his clan to achieve that distinction, the event carried special meaning and responsibility. He represented the whole family. He was going to stand for something. He illustrated the great American dream.

College had been good for Vince. He really hadn't chosen Northwestern State Teachers College. When you grew up in the rural towns, the son of a gypsum miner or a wheat farmer, your choice was to go to college or to go to the City and try to get on with the fire department. And if you chose college, you went to the one nearest you where you mingled with other kids from small towns who had gone to the same high schools and who now plunged themselves into the same activities and purposes. And if you were average or athletic or both, you stretched your vision as far as the elastic of dreams would allow and prepared for a life as a teacher and a coach.

For Vince, graduation came as a paradox, an anticlimax, a little piece of hazy reality wedged into the wholeness of real life. He hadn't planned for it to be that way. He had actually planned to save up for the event, to conserve both senses and emotions so he could celebrate the achievement as something consequential, bigger than anything which had ever happened to him before, and then to celebrate with all his consciousness on full speed.

But one month to the day before his college graduation, Vince's father died. Papa Benalli was a man of many descriptions, but chief among them was happy. Cheerful and smiling, he was a great practical joker who had a sense of humor big enough to allow him to love everybody. Not only did he enjoy living, but he made life richer for those around him.

When he was a young man, he had migrated from the coal mines of Pennsylvania to the gypsum hills of Oklahoma, and he had changed his career from digging the black fuel from deep inside the earth to harvesting the white gypsum rock which seemed to grow on the crest of the hills around Canton. Operating a special machine, he loaded the soft rock into trucks which hauled it to the plant where it was ground into powder to be pressed into wallboard. For a real miner, that kind of activity would have seemed out of place; but for him, the son of an Italian immigrant, it was still close enough to mining to satisfy the family vocational heritage.

Once in Oklahoma, Papa Benalli had no choice except to take on the prairie ways, but he had the wit to decorate those ways with Italian charm. He married an Oklahoma girl, a farmer's daughter, and in Old World fashion they raised seven children, concluding with son Vincent. Urged by his wife, he joined the Baptist church, and through the years, he became a deacon. But the family always seemed to have more customs than their neighbors, especially at religious times of the year such as Easter and Christmas.

In short, he was a happy Oklahoma Italian until the night he suddenly died. At suppertime, while talking about some humorous event which had happened at the quarry, he stopped in the middle of a sentence and died, just months before his fiftieth birthday.

The shock wore gaps in Vince's world that all the awkward stabs of sympathy couldn't touch. He had lost a father and a friend, someone who had set the rhythm for living life to its limit, regardless of circumstances. But he had also lost a counselor. For years, Vince had not really actively asked for his father's advice and might not have even taken it, had his father offered. But after a decision was made—a car was bought, a course was chosen, or the girl proposed to—Vince went immediately for Papa's blessing. Now, Vince had to make his own decisions, and he couldn't even ask, "What will Papa bless and what will he not bless?"

Despite his age, Vince was also astute enough to know that when he lost Papa, he lost the family as well. He had watched the six older brothers and sisters grow independent and further from that magic circle which was the family. But they always came back because their lives spun around the hub which was Papa. But now that the hub had disintegrated into dust, the spokes would fly apart, never to quite come together as a family again.

At times, during the month between Papa's death and his graduation, Vince felt that he might set his world right again if he could just answer one question. "Why did I work so hard to graduate, if Papa can't be here to see me?"

At college, Vince had majored in English and he had played

basketball; and he was good at both. The same feistiness and determination which made him the smallest all-conference player also made him a tenacious student of literature. He liked basketball—it was the game of the young. He loved literature—it was the game of life.

And he used that thought to give himself youthful assurance when he drove into Wheatheart that spring afternoon of 1957, just two weeks after graduation. "They need a basketball coach, and I think maybe an English teacher," his college coach had said. "I've recommended you. Why don't you go down and check it out. That's a good little community. I think you can handle it."

But now as he headed his college-worn car up Main Street to the high school, he wasn't so sure. There was something about this little town that looked more complicated than he had expected. Somewhere in the bowels of this community, there was a mystique which fascinated him. He knew a few things about the place already—he had known some natives at school, football players mostly, and he learned more driving through.

Like most of the towns on the high prairie, Wheatheart grew out of the horizon. From a distance, with only the grain elevators in sight, it looked like a place for the local farmers to dump wheat; but closer in, the town took on a distinct personality. Casual visitors and passers-through would not have noticed it; but Vince, having grown up in one of the country towns, saw it immediately. The two banks spoke of prosperity. The farmers here were good ones, and probably stable. This would be a place where a man could make some dreams. The thriving hospital, so unusual for isolated towns of this size, spoke of independence. Years ago, some doctor had set up shop in Wheatheart, and had stayed. Now, people did not have to go off to observe the rituals of living and dying. They could get born and die and live all their lives in-between and never have to leave town. The churches, with the Baptist Church standing authoritatively in charge, the Methodist Church sitting reverently among a cedar hedge, and the other churches, Pentecostal, Seventh Day Adventist, and Church of Christ, looking temporary in the converted store fronts up and down Main Street, spoke of a powerful moral code based on man's most hopeful search. Duty was an expression of worship here. In this town, a young teacher could assign homework and know that students would do it, whether they wanted to or not.

The high school, sitting on top of the hill at the end of Main Street, spoke of community. The school was the heart of Wheatheart and gave the town a sense of pride and direction. Here teachers and coaches—the two were often synonymous—would be more than mere public servants relegated to anonymity. They would be known, integral agents in civic affairs and town distinction. Never mind the chuckholes in the streets or the peeling paint on the highway side of the drugstore, or the height of the weeds in the vacant lots, or the firetruck which never starts. How did the ball team do? "That well, eh? We sure have a great little town, don't we?"

The whole tour didn't take Vince long—one short pass along the highway and one short trip up Main Street, all the way from the John Deere place on the south to the high school at the north end; but he learned a lot by looking fast, so he was ready for his interview with Mr. Casteel, the superintendent. Although a relatively young man, Mr. Casteel was already a five-year veteran at his post as head of community unity, and he wore the job with an air of permanence. "You had better like this guy," Vince thought. "He is here to stay."

"Well, what do you think of our little town?" The question was wrapped in a down-home friendliness, outwardly designed to make Vince comfortable for the tougher ones to follow. But even this one had purpose. In fact, after the interview was all over, Vince knew this might have been the most important question.

"I like what I see. Very clean. Looks prosperous. What's the population here?" An education professor had told Vince to ask some questions of his own during these interviews. It gave the superintendent the impression that you were discriminating, even if you were prepared to take the first job offered, even in Timbuktu.

"About 1,240 in town itself, but our district covers another 1,000 or so. We go all the way to the river on the north and east." He had answered this question before, so this was just recitation. "We have about 175 high school kids, give or take a few. We're mostly a farming economy, wheat. And we do well when it rains and struggle during the dry years. I guess we are about like a lot of districts around here." He laughed, but it was a chuckle of condescension! They certainly weren't like the other districts! Even if they were, in some respects, Vince knew he had better see the difference. This man was doing him an honor just to interview him, and Vince should appreciate it as such.

"Are you expecting any growth?" Vince shouldn't have asked that question. It was not only dumb, for he knew the answer; it was also in poor taste—a direct attack on that condescending laugh. Farm communities don't grow; they don't have to. Growth is for weak places, unstable places that haven't defined their distinctives yet. Growth would only weaken Wheatheart. Transients can't help you much. Vince knew the question was wrong when he asked, and he deserved the reprimand in the answer.

"No, not really, but let's talk about you." Mr. Casteel was more embarrassed for Vince than for himself. "What was your major?"

"English."

"Good. Excellent. We really put a lot of stock in our English teacher here. That is an important subject, maybe the most important, in my way of thinking. If you can't talk, there isn't much you can do, I've always said. Gotta learn to communicate if you ever expect to amount to anything."

"Yes, sir. And. . . ."

"And another thing, our English teacher is the one person who sees them all. Every student takes English, so you might say that the English teacher sets the tone for the whole school. Give me a good English teacher, and this whole place runs better. But if the English teacher lets them walk all over him, then they will walk all over everybody else. Yes, sir. That is an important job. You think you're man enough to handle it?"

"Well, I have really enjoyed my study. I like to write, and I enjoy bringing literature to life, at least in my own life. And. . ."

"That's good. What about your basketball? You made all-conference, it says."

"Yes. I squeezed in a little time for basketball during my studies."

"Hey, I saw you play once."

"Really?"

"Sure did. When you were in high school, state tournament game. You were playing, let's see, that's been a few years ago. I've slept since then. You were playing Durant, I believe, or some town down east."

Lately, Vince had been too busy building bridges into the future to spend much time linking to the past; he couldn't immediately identify that moment in Mr. Casteel's memory, so he just sat back and listened.

"You sure put on a show that night. You must have stole the ball fifteen times, and you carried the scoring. Best defensive hustle I can remember seeing."

Vince wished he could help with the picture. Obviously, it had made an impression. But that kid playing a wild, reckless game five years ago was someone else, a figure in Vince's distant past. He knew him once, but not anymore. Somewhere during college, that kid passed on and left his legacy to a man more deliberate and thoughtful than the kid could have ever been. He realized that he sat in that interview under false pretense. Mr. Casteel thought that Vince was the same person he had seen play in some insignificant basketball game five years ago. Now, Mr. Casteel looked at a grown man with promise and a future and saw only a cocky kid who lived once years ago. Vince was confused, but deeper down he was challenged. "Give me the opportunity," he thought, "and I will correct that misconception."

Mr. Casteel continued, "As you know, Vince, we need a basketball coach. Someone like you. Someone who can come in here and teach our kids how to hustle. We got a lot of promise in this little town, a lot of future here. We got a good football program—a fine young coach, A.G. Rose—but we need someone to take those same old kids and turn them into basketball players during the winter. Someone to teach our kids to play that game just like you did. I like the way you look. I think you can do us a job here. What do you think?''

It had gone faster than Vince had even hoped. "Well, what about the English?''

"Oh, that's part of it, all right. You will teach four classes of high school English and coach junior high and high school basketball. We'll keep you pretty busy. Any questions?''

"Well, I think so.''

"Sure you do. As you probably know, we play in the Shortgrass Conference—Shattuck, Tonkawa, Mooreland, and Eagle City. Teams like that. Of course, we just naturally plan a late start here. Our football team has been getting in the play-offs every year lately. So we start basketball late. But you will have lots of kids.''

"Yes, I know all that, but. . . .''

"Well, I am not going to tell you how to run your team. No one will here. We support our coaches. That's the way we are. But I sure like that man-to-man defense the way you played it in high school. Not telling you, understand, but just making a suggestion.''

"But what about the English?''

"Oh, don't worry about our old kids in class. Mostly country kids. They're pretty easy to control. That's what makes them such good athletes. Discipline. They will do what you tell them. We've got a pretty good bunch around here. Lots of support from the community. Good turnout and all.''

"Yes, but have they ever heard of Shakespeare, or Wordsworth, or even Thoreau?'' Vince thought it, but he didn't dare ask it. He just sat across the table from Mr. Casteel and tried hard to dream past what he had just heard.

"Got a family, Vince?''

Now that was a question he could get into. "Yes, I have a wife. Elizabeth Ann. Beth Ann. We have been married almost a year. No children yet. She will graduate too.''

"Teacher?"

"No, she majored in business, but she is more interested in motherhood right now."

"Good. You shouldn't have any trouble finding a place to live, and our contract is. . . ." And with that, the day droned into routine: contracts, houses for rent, starting days, gym floors, uniforms, and finally, English books.

When it was all over, Vince was too shocked to be weary. Heading east out of town, he drove to the top of half-mile hill and pulled his car to the side of the road. Turning and looking out the back glass, he surveyed his new home where he and Beth Ann would settle and make babies and plans and dreams, where it would all come true someday.

From where he sat now, the trees were thicker and greener than he had noticed when he drove in; the elevators were taller and cleaner, and the school hill was bigger and more prominent. The eight football light poles he hadn't seen before cast long shadows in the spring sun.

As his eyes surveyed the town, his mind surveyed the day, as best as it could.

Recently, change had come in leaps—college, marriage, a new job. Leaps are nice, a good way to grow. And death—he had forgotten death—his father's. At least for the moment, he had forgotten, and it felt good to forget. But he couldn't forever, and that thought stood behind the present moment—blinking on and off its warning that in spite of his youth, his dreams, his hunger, and his leaps, there would always be things he couldn't take charge of, couldn't make happen, no matter how hard he tried or believed.

The urge to get back to Alva and tell Beth Ann the news of the next leap cut his survey short. Regardless of the thoughts in his soul, he still had life to live. But before he drove on, he made time for one last chore. More than a chore, a duty; but more than a duty. From inside his coat pocket, he pulled a small spiral book and a graduation gift pen. He flipped through the pages until he found the first blank, and he wrote in a style which added to his small collection.

> My Father in heaven:
> Though I can't see the other side,
> I trust You across the chasm.
> Though I can't know You like You know me,
> may we both agree.
> And may I not cheat our opportunity.

Twenty-three years later, as Vince sat among the cobwebs and stale dust of a dimly lit basement room in Wheatheart High School, he recalled it all. He retained the sights and the sounds as vividly as when they had happened. But somewhere, in the rapid race of becoming forty-six, he had lost the smells, the tastes, the feelings, and the reasons. Just as the first whiffs of breakfast destroy last night's dream you were trying to keep, real life had chased his dreams too far away for them to come back.

Since he couldn't be young again, not even in his memories, he had to be the principal.

A Chance To Forget
1980

The clanging bell upstairs filtered through the floor but still made enough racket to disturb Vince out of his memory and back into the present. He turned off the light, climbed the stairs, and casually, in feigned ignorance, ambled down the hall toward his office where he already knew what he would find.

"Where have you been? We've got a crisis here." Miss Helen McClurg had been the high school secretary for sixteen years. She was ideal for the spot. She could run both the high school and the community and never leave herself unprotected to accept responsibility for anything which went wrong. Although she didn't enjoy her work too much, she loved her post—Busybody in Charge.

"Why? What happened?" On most days in this situation, she would have been the principal and Vince would have been the little boy in trouble, and he would have attempted some awkward alibi about his strange disappearance. But not today. He just didn't feel like playing that game. He didn't owe her any explanation.

"Well," she went on with eagerness, "Craig Brady and Bobby Golden were fighting, beating each other to death down in the south hall. Mr. Goddard caught them. He was down fixing a light in

Mrs. Bell's room and he heard them. Lucky he was there. No telling what might have happened. Nobody in the hall—those two strong boys just pounding on each other. It could have really been bad, I tell you. But he caught them and brought them down here.''

"Any blood?" Someday Vince had to learn that Miss McClurg had absolutely no sense of humor. Today, her stare was enough to remind him. So he decided he didn't need any more of that conversation. He opened the door and went on into his office where the two boys sat on opposite sides of the room staring at the floor, with their arms clasped in front of them.

Bobby Golden, the senior and starting halfback, was competent but not great; yet he would receive some distinction in the Wheatheart football legends simply because the team would probably win the state championship. He was from one of the newer families of Wheatheart; they had come up from somewhere in the southeast part of the state to help build the new elevator, ten, maybe fifteen years ago, and had just stayed on to work around town when it was finished. Craig Brady was a junior, small but tough, and from one of the oldest families in town. His grandfather was something of a town character, a real storyteller who had a Mark Twain charm about him, except he kept telling the same stories over and over.

Vince wandered between the boys and took his seat behind the desk. He had read those management books which recommended sitting out in front of his desk so there wouldn't be any barriers. But in the principal's office, the barriers were already there and everybody knew it. He was the authority and the kids were in trouble. Why play games with that arrangement? He sat silently for several seconds and inspected the damages. Bobby's shirt was twisted and wrinkled at the collar and the top buttonhole had been ripped out. Craig had a red welt just below his right cheekbone, a bit too low to promise much of a shiner, but a good-looking war wound, nevertheless.

"I hear you guys have been fighting."

"No. We weren't fighting."

"We're good friends. We wouldn't fight."

Those answers didn't surprise Vince. Nothing heals the chasms of youth as quickly as having an outsider step between. Regardless of what separates them, authority can almost always drive them together.

"Why were you in the hall?"

"Well, we had something to talk over. We talked about it at lunch and decided to meet to talk about it."

"Yeah. We were just talking."

"What about?" Vince was having trouble keeping the smile out of the corner of his eyes.

"Well, it was . . ."

"It was personal."

"Yeah. It was personal."

"You don't want to tell me then?" Vince tried to make that sound like a threat with consequences.

"We would rather not say."

"What happened to your shirt, Bobby?" Vince knew, and the boys knew that he knew. But they still expected him to ask.

"Oh, that! Well, we were pushing each other around at lunch. Trying to push someone outside, I ripped it."

"Who?"

"Well, you know. The guys."

"What about the eye, Craig?"

"I ran into the door of the bathroom."

"Beg your pardon?" Though he had heard it so many times before, he still couldn't get ready for that.

"Well, I ran into the door of the bathroom. They won't let us back in the hall at noon until the first bell rings, and then we get an unexcused tardy if we aren't in our seats when the second bell rings. There just isn't enough time if you have to stop and go to the bathroom. I think they ought to do something about that."

Vince admired his answer. Already Craig had his grandfather's flair for storytelling. That sixteen-year-old had just turned from defense to offense right in the middle of his own trial. It was definitely an inspired move. Vince wished he had more time to appreciate it. This young man had promise.

"Craig, have you ever heard discretion is the better part of valor?"

"No, sir. Was that a hit song in the fifties?"

Vince had already been feeling his age all day long and he didn't need any more reminders, so he changed the tone. "Well, what about it? 'Be sure your sin will find you out.' "

"Oh, I know about that, sir. I have already asked Jesus to take my sins away."

Bobby didn't want to be outdone in this conversation, and he was beginning to grow a bit suspicious. "Me too, but I didn't think we were supposed to talk about that in school. Our preacher told us that it was against the law to talk religion in schools."

Since Bobby's attempt at offense was not as clean as Craig's had been, Vince figured that he was getting close to a confession. "It's all right in here, Bobby. I just want you guys to know the facts before we go on . . ."

Suddenly, there were two pounds on the door and Mr. Casteel came barging in. He could do that. He was the superintendent. He was entitled to inspect all problems and listen to all conversations. He had the right to know, and to interfere. To him, subtlety and chewing gum were human weaknesses.

"Miss McClurg told me these guys were fighting. What are you going to do about it, Mr. Benalli?"

"Well, first, I am going to try to figure out what happened."

"I never saw the like—fighting, this week of all weeks! I don't know what you guys can be thinking about. Beats all I ever saw. Here we are about to play for the championship of the entire state of Oklahoma and you guys have the nerve to jeopardize it by banging on each other. That's a pretty selfish act, don't you think?"

"Yes, sir."

There wasn't any offense in either answer. This time, the confessions poured out through outward signs of guilt—flushed faces, bowed heads, and clasped hands. Even Vince felt it, and all three guilty parties, the boys and Vince, braced for more lecture.

"You're not just in this thing for yourself. You owe something to this community, to the school, to your parents, for heaven's sake. If you are too pigheaded to make good decisions on your own, you ought at least to think about the other people involved. Now what do you think this kind of thing is going to do to our team? Or is that something you haven't thought about? Well, I don't know what Mr. Benalli is going to do, but if he suspends both of you for three days, we're going to be up a creek, come Friday night. I'll promise you that. Were you thinking suspension, Mr. Benalli?"

"No, sir. I had not thought about suspension." And that was the truth. The thought had never crossed his mind. Maybe once, years ago, he would have thought about it, but not now. When he was young and still had dreams, he might have believed that he could change things. Use the opportunity. Make things better. Make these boys better, more mature and more eager. Make the whole school better, more humane and sensitive. But he wasn't young anymore, and he didn't believe those things. Once, maybe fifteen years ago, he had believed in suspension, had demanded it, in fact. He had broken up a fight in the south hall, almost in the same place. He was a teacher then, still working for that just world that had to be right around the corner. So he used his clout to demand justice, suspension; and the two young men, children at heart and play, went home for three days to try to grow up. Nine months later, one of them was shot down in a helicopter over Vietnam. At the memorial service at the gym, with all of Wheatheart turned out to celebrate a fallen hero, and to feel good about themselves for having made such a contribution to national security, Vince read the appropriate poetry, Kilmer's "I Have a Rendezvous with Death" and wondered what it meant to be grown-up and just. No, he had not thought about suspension this time.

It didn't matter. Mr. Casteel hadn't heard his answer anyway, and couldn't have understood if he had heard. "Well, I tell you what I think I would do if I were you, Mr. Benalli. I think I would get Coach Rose in here. He needs to know about this. He is not going to like what he hears. I can assure you of that. Yeah. Get Coach Rose. He will know what to do." And with that, Mr. Casteel left as abruptly as he had come, off to solve other problems.

In spite of how it sounded, this was more than a suggestion; it was an order; Vince sent Miss McClurg to find the coach. The three of them waited silently, each beaten deep into his own thoughts by the pounding of wind and grit against the windows. In a different place, Vince might have enjoyed the company of these two young men, naively bright and athletic. But not today. His authority separated them. And it wasn't really his own authority at that. It was Casteel's decision, Casteel's presence which built the walls between Vince and those two students, caught in the act of being kids. Something inside Vince wanted to reach out and smash that wall to oblivion. And then the three of them could start all over again with their little game of questions and answers, humoring each other but learning at the same time.

But something else inside him, something that seemed almost holy, wouldn't even let him think that thought—at least, not for long. So there he sat, not even as an actor who frets and struts his time upon the stage, but as a reactor, a puppet dancing on the ends of a string. In that office, in that mood, he was an authority figure, all right, but there was always someone or something else supplying the authority—Casteel, the office, or even the image of the office. But it was never his own wants or needs. And that drained him dry, always guessing what he got from someone else rather than what he created inside himself. He was worn to exhaustion by emptiness. Besides, he was forty-six.

"Mr. Benalli, you want to see me?" Coach Rose was always efficiently gracious, but he was also always Coach Rose.

"Coach, these two good friends here were having a rather loud discussion down in the south hall. Maybe they were discussing how rough it is just being a student here. In the course of the conversation, Bobby got his shirt torn, and old Craig, there, was attacked by the bathroom door."

"I'm not surprised. These two have had a lot of things to talk about lately, I've noticed. There seems to be some misunderstanding between them about territorial rights." Coach Rose never seemed interested in the personal lives of the students, but he always knew such things. "I think maybe I can come up with a solution. Let me design some activities for them after practice today, give them a chance to spend some time together. I think maybe ten laps around the practice field might just give them enough time to talk this thing out. Then it will all be in the past and we can get on with the business at hand. What do you think, guys?"

"Yes, sir." Momentarily, they were relieved. Since the tone had changed from the Casteel regime only moments earlier, the punishment didn't seem so severe. In a different situation, ten extra laps would have produced some groans. But not this time. They were just glad Mr. Casteel had left. Almost eagerly, they got up and went back to class, leaving Vince and the coach alone to predict the outcome.

Vince spoke first. "Thanks, Coach. I appreciate your taking care of this, but I am not really sure it is a team matter."

"Maybe not, Vincent, but around here maybe everything is a team matter. It's hard to tell the difference, isn't it? Well, at least, those experts down at the Dew Drop Inn will think we are taking care of things up here. It ought to satisfy them. And running never hurts a kid. Thanks for inviting me in."

He stopped in midthought and fixed his stare and his mind somewhere else. Since this was usual for Coach Rose and since he was Coach Rose, he could do that. He wasn't being rude. He was just pausing to formulate a thought—a thought worth thinking or at least one that would bring another dimension to the matter at hand.

Since Vince knew this, he didn't interrupt. In fact, he enjoyed the break. In conversation with Rose, he enjoyed the quiet time to look inside himself. With Rose he enjoyed it, but not with anyone else. Besides, Rose always called him Vincent, just as Papa used to.

Finally, Rose spoke.

"How many times have we done this, Vincent?"

The principal laughed. "Somewhere between ten and a thousand."

Rose, the man, not the coach, spoke again with feeling but not impatience. "Do we ever get it right—the way we want it?"

Now it was Vince's time to pause, to take advantage of the consent between the two which was strong enough to permit and even provoke silence. In the stillness of the room with the wind gusting forcefully against the window, Vince fussed with two answers, both questions really, but answers. One was appropriate and thoughtful and simply profound. The other was honest, but too honest, even now too honest.

"How will we ever know?" Vince asked, with a sigh which shook his whole body, and hid the unspoken answer which he couldn't say aloud just now or ever, not even in the presence of his best friend. But he thought about it. Like a sticker festering in the bottom of your foot during a waterskiing weekend, that other answer lay underneath the mental surface and pricked Vince just enough to mar the complete happiness of any moment. And he hated himself for thinking it, but never finding the courage to say it—"What difference does it make if we get it right or not? In the long run, when we grow old and they grow up, what difference will this make?"

Maybe Rose understood. Maybe that was what he was asking too, underneath his words. But Vince would never know, because those are the kinds of things you can only know about yourself and tell yourself.

The coach left Vince's office looking as if he still had something to say—but then he always looked that way.

Alone again, Vince invested his emotions into another thought, trying to figure out where he stood in relation to those structures that surrounded him, structures of friendships and work and duty and wife and church and God Himself. Those structures which were supposed to free him were actually pulling him down, and he wasn't sure he knew why.

Oh, he understood some of it, all right. He understood his relationship with Casteel. That was obvious. And since he understood, the whole thing didn't bother him that much. He knew what role he had to play, a role he had created by his own past decisions.

But Coach Rose was different. They were best friends. At least, Vince would call Rose his best friend, his only professional confidant. Although they never spent that much time together, especially during football season, they were still best friends. Yet, even in the company of Rose, Vince couldn't find the courage to be honest, and he didn't know why. He wanted to know. He wanted to pry into this until he made meaning of loneliness. He wanted to remember how he came to feel alone in the presence of his best friend.

But that puzzle would have to wait because the last bell was about to ring, and he wanted to be in the hall when the students passed through on their way to the other activities which filled their day and their dreams. Besides, Vince welcomed the chance to forget himself and his feelings.

What Difference Does It Make?
1980, 1960

This was Vince's favorite time of the day. He couldn't explain it, not even to himself, but somehow that clanging bell turned sweet at 3:30 and his office changed. Or maybe he changed the office and became something other than Mr. Benalli, the high school principal.

He was still Mr. Benalli, all right—to the teachers as well as the students—but it was a Mr. Benalli of a different tone. Now the requirements of school were over and the after-school rituals began.

Almost all the students stayed for the rituals—the activities and games of youth—extracurricular activities in other places but not at Wheatheart. These activities weren't extra; they never had been. They were the reason the school stood on that hill and the reason the daily Dew Drop Inn conversation always included time for such topics as state championship games and fights in the hall.

Not all the students stayed for the rituals—cheerleading, F.F.A., football, band, speech, science fair. Some, the weaker students mostly and the isolates, went home to chores or TV. But most stayed and relaxed into excitement.

"Hi, Mr. Benalli."

"Have a nice evening, Mr. Benalli."

"Mr. Benalli, did anyone find a cheerleading skirt? I lost mine somewhere."

"Are you coming out to football practice, Mr. Benalli?"

"Mr. Benalli, will the building be open tonight? We want to decorate the guys' lockers, and we don't have the footballs cut out yet."

"Mr. Benalli, if my mother comes for me, tell her that I am going home with Donna Faye to practice our twirling routine."

"When do the buses leave for the City on Friday, Mr. Benalli?"

"Mr. Benalli, Mrs. Fisher wanted me to ask you when we should put out the next issue of the paper."

"Mr. Benalli, you look so calm. Aren't you just a little bit excited about this week?"

"Mr. Benalli, will you ask your wife if the bank wants to buy a full-page ad for the yearbook? If they do, maybe we could run color in the football section this year. Don't you agree?"

"Hi, Mr. Benalli."

"Bye, Mr. Benalli."

"Shoot, the wind's blowin'."

"Oh, good, the wind's blowing. We won't have to punt in practice tonight."

Mostly, Vince offered them facts, when he had them; but when facts weren't enough, he offered them wise words which could have been wisdom if Vince had only known what they meant.

"Will you be happy when we win State, Mr. Benalli?"

Vince couldn't answer the question, not truthfully. For one thing, he didn't know the truth; and if he had known the truth, he would have been afraid of it. But he could lecture. He never passed up a chance to lecture. He was the principal, and that meant he was the principal teacher at Wheatheart High School; it also meant he lectured when the opportunity came. "Happiness is what you are and not something you earn," he repeated in his finest "I am the principal and you are a student" tones.

"We are really going to have fun after we win State, Mr. Benalli."

More lecture. "Fun is in the getting and not in the having."

"Mr. Benalli, do you think that poets, any creative people, are inspired, the way the people who wrote the Bible were?"

The question should not have surprised Vince. He had seen Jimmy Charles Ericson coming down the hall, and Jimmy Charles had surprised him so often that he wasn't surprised by the boy's surprises anymore. And the question was as sincere as it was mature. Jimmy Charles was not just marking time and passing through. He was a football player who had to hurry to practice, but first he had to work on this idea as if it were a sore sharp enough to demand immediate salve.

And Vince couldn't soothe that sore with lecture. It required something more honest. Jimmy Charles had presented a piece of himself, maybe all of himself, to ask the question. In the presence of Mr. Benalli, he stood vulnerable, emotionally naked, pleading almost aloud a humble confession, "I am ignorant and you know. Please teach me."

So Vince spoke, not as a teacher nor a principal but as one human being to another as the two joined spirits, like two uncut stalks of wheat standing tall and untouched by machines and practicality in the middle of a plowed field. They dug deep into the ways of man and the mind of God and talked about things of the soul which no one else in Wheatheart talked about during the week of the state championship. They were good for each other, those two standing alone in an active hall, so busy in thought that they did not even hear the wind and the dirt bang the north door open and shut.

And all the while, Vince never once remembered that this was Jimmy Charles Ericson, second-string halfback, who would have started Friday night if Bobby Golden had been suspended for fighting in the halls. And Jimmy Charles either didn't know or didn't care about his missed opportunity. And since he didn't, Vince forgot to think his question, "What difference does it make?" Forgot, that is, until Jimmy Charles had to dash off to take his part in the rituals of Wheatheart honor as a second-string halfback.

In his absence, Vince stood in the hall all alone and listened to the drone.

"Hi, Mr. Benalli."

"Mr. Benalli, may I use the phone to call my mother?"

"Mr. Benalli, will we have to do the play the first Friday in December, even if we don't get our lines learned?"

"Tom took my purse and he won't give it back, Mr. Benalli."

"Hi, Mr. Benalli."

"Bye, Mr. Benalli."

When the hall traffic let up, Vince wandered back into his office, shut the door, and sat down at his desk. With nothing else to do, he searched the past to try to remember why he couldn't look Coach Rose squarely in the eye and say, "What difference does it make?"

Protected from the outside activities by windows and walls and his own memory, Vince reviewed his Wheatheart career as if he were a literary critic searching for a clue to some hidden truth he had never seen before.

He had been over the story several times before, particularly since he had turned forty-six; but he kept reviewing, searching, hoping to find that one point which would tell him what difference it makes.

As usual, he started the search with basketball, going back to 1960. . . .

At best, coaching basketball was like being married to a fickle spouse. Through sheer determination and devotion (sometimes the two look exactly alike), you took the good with the bad and counted your blessings by saying, "Well, it could be worse."

At Wheatheart, for young Vince Benalli, coaching basketball was like David attacking Goliath with cotton balls in a windstorm. If he timed the gusts right, he might hope to make a sport out of it. But if his timing was lousy, it all blew back in his face and pestered him.

It wasn't as if Vince was a bad coach. He was a good coach, in fact. His teams played well. The players usually performed with regulated outbursts of enthusiasm mixed with skill, and during his eleven years they won more basketball games than at any other period in Wheatheart history. Yet, football saturated the town and leaked out through all the cracks. It was more than a seasonal pastime, more than something to accommodate the fall promise of starting school and planting a new crop. Football was an all-consuming way of life, the topic just below the surface of any conversation between any two people in town, whether they liked the game or not. From August 15, when the boys of the community first donned the leather and tape armors and endured the hot, late summer sun and the endless character-building running and banging, until early December, when those same young men, now grown into seasoned athletes measured their training and integrity against the finest in the state, the football passion was intense. Games, pep rallies, Quarterback Club meetings—official and unofficial, team dinners, injury reports, progress reports, banners, storefront window decorations, post-game celebrations and parties, all took on the air of consummate importance and provided the whole community with a common "other" around which all lives and all life could revolve. Football was more than something the community shared together. It *was* the community.

Vince was smart enough not to tilt with the community windmill. You can tilt with your own personal windmills if you want, chase your own fantasies and dreams, so that when you make a fool out of yourself you'll be the only one who knows. But don't mess with a community obsession.

So in the beginning, he didn't fight the force of football; he joined it. He took as active a role as he could without jeopardizing his own distinctives.

He helped in the training room, visited practices, scouted on Friday nights, joined the celebration parties, attended the quarterback meetings, and participated in the analysis and prophecy conversations at the Dew Drop Inn or the grocery store. Vince was also astute enough as a young teacher to know not to combat football spirit in class, so he constructed his whole schedule to accommodate game-day jitters. He devoted every fall Friday to poetry reading. At first he began those sessions with the classic battle cries, the kind of stuff which might have been appropriate for hanging in dressing rooms. But gradually, he moved into the more profound and imaginative work, leaving the students, at least those who listened, with some sense of a world larger than Whippet Field and a destiny beyond the final minute of the fourth quarter.

And through all this, Vince was Coach Rose's closest friend, but sometimes at a distance. Since he was so involved with the program, he and the coach talked often and Vince looked forward to those conversations. On the surface, Rose was bigger than life. Although he was only just over five ten, veteran players and fans would often bet that he was at least six two. In all his days of watching practice, Vince never heard him speak above his normal tone of voice; yet players would often brag about being yelled at by the coach. When Rose was in charge, the practices were harder, the sun hotter, the laps longer, the learning clearer, and the victories sweeter than they would have been if anybody else had been coaching. As soon as he started, the man was a legend. And maybe it was this romantic legend which Vince sought and found so appealing. He liked being near the man. For some reason, when he was around this legend, he took on the air of greatness himself, but where only he knew. Somehow he became wittier, and more astute, and more under-standing, and somehow just a little more contented with the way things really were in all of Wheatheart.

But after a while, the pressure of being nice wore Vince thin. Football was too constant. He could have lived his role as helper for part of the year, and it wouldn't have even been a lie. But not all the time, not constantly. He was just not that unselfish or one-dimen-sional. There were days when *he* needed the attention, when *he* needed the community support, when *he* needed to be the source of a legend himself.

But it never came. The town wasn't malicious—the parents, players, fans, even Coach Rose; they were just preoccupied. Regard-less of how hard Vince worked or dreamed, he never got more than second best. The little things, comments made in passing, never meant to hurt, dug deep into his spirit and decision-making.

"I'll sure be glad when this football season is over. Maybe I'll have my son home nights again."

"Let's not schedule the play during football when everyone is so busy."

"Howja do last night, Vince? We stayed home and watched that new program on TV."

"Roger is playing good basketball for a sophomore. I never knew he was that aggressive. He may have a real future as a defensive back come next fall."

Finally, it all got to him and he just couldn't take it any longer. It wasn't as if he made an active decision, like buying a new car or taking a book out of the library. But gradually, he withdrew from the football passion. He quit going to practices and quit helping; more emphatically, he started resenting the whole thing. One day he woke up to the shocking realization that he even wanted the team to lose. He resented their success and their complete domination of the community. And when he realized that, the pressure really built up because he couldn't tell anybody. A genuine thought, a genuine attitude, and he had to keep it all to himself, and act as if it weren't so. He almost resented himself for resenting football. Yet he continued to coach his basketball team with fervor and enthusiasm, and no one ever suspected that he was unpatriotic or maybe even heretical.

But in the midst of all this, he still looked forward to his times with Coach Rose. And that was the mystery which bothered him the most. Surely, Rose must have noticed that Vince's support had cooled, but he never said anything. The conversations and the friendship continued. It didn't grow or get thicker or more intimate or more time-consuming—it just continued on the same even path, and Vince felt strange about that too. Deep down in the crevices of his own soul where all people spend time alone, where pacts are made with God and where real human love lives, Vince hated the coach, or at least hated his image. But he enjoyed their time together. This paradox trapped him. He knew it wasn't honest, but it was real.

The event which locked them tightest together, both in time and space, was the annual statewide coaching clinic. For five days in early August, coaches throughout the state gathered in either Oklahoma City or Tulsa and spent at least part of each day in meetings and seminars discussing the finer points of zone defense and pass blocking. Although Rose and Vince went with different interests and attended different sessions, they nonetheless went together and lived together for the whole five days. And they were thrown even closer together through mutual interests and lifestyles. For many of the coaches, it was their annual time to escape the oppression of the small-town grapevine and judgment, and to experience the quickened heartbeat of life in the fast lane. After each day's work diet of diagrams and discussions, they traveled in herds from bar to bar and nightspot to nightspot, engaging in any activity which seemed brazen or urbane. Conscientious men, moral leaders of the youth of the community, men who from September to May preached discipline and responsibility to impressionable youth, threw caution to the hot August wind and suspended their own rules for one week a year.

But not Vince or Coach Rose. For Vince, it was the matter of a pact. He had promised his soul to God and he chose to keep his word. Although Rose never discussed it with anyone, his restraint seemed to be a matter of judgment. Such behavior just didn't make sense. That's all.

So each evening, the two men, separated from their colleagues by preference, dined together, walked a bit, perhaps took in a movie, and talked intensely if not thoroughly.

One night after dinner, they lay quietly in their hotel beds, tuned into the noises of the city and fascinated by the flashing beats of light flowing from the neon signs designed to entice and thrill. Somehow the regular rhythms of the lights and sounds beat themselves into artificial silence and darkness, and Vince was caught with an impelling need to be honest, to tell this man—less than a legend now in the almost darkened room—of the rivalry which kept their friendship a paradox. This was his opportunity, Vince thought, to take the risk, to lay himself bare and paint the facade with reality. It was a risk, but regardless of how it went, he would still be relieved. Rose might have been the wisest man he knew, and at this point,

Vince needed some wise counsel. Why not get the solution from the man inside the problem?

"Coach?" Vince's voice sounded hollow against the background of street sounds.

"Yes?"

"What's the bravest act a man could do?" It wasn't really a strange question for these two. They often played these kinds of mental games.

"That's easy. You thought I would say, 'Die for a cause,' but I am not sure that takes any great courage. Cowards die for causes. They get caught up in the spirit of the moment fired by some fanatic speech or loud music or even some abstract notion of patriotism or duty. I don't understand why it works, but it does. I guess some would say that that is the secret of coaching. Take some ordinary kid and fire him up until he gets brave enough to do the job. It works, though it sure doesn't say much for the human being, does it?"

"I've never thought of it like that, but I guess not. But you didn't answer my question."

"Ask me again. These city lights cause my mind to wander."

"Be careful how far it wanders. I don't want to lose my room-mate here in the middle of the night. . . . What is the bravest thing a man can do?"

The time of Vince's wait for the answer was magnified by the imposing city which made him even more aware of the man lying in the other bed. Rose's voice was almost a whisper. "Live the truth."

"So what is so tough about telling the truth?"

"I didn't say *tell* the truth. I said *live* the truth."

Vince had heard what he wanted to hear rather than what Rose had said, and he remembered the paradox which had prompted the conversation in the first place. He decided to pursue the course to see if he could direct it where he wanted it to go. "What's the difference?"

This time he understood the silence. Rose was formulating an answer. "Vincent, do you remember Seneca?"

"Who?"

"Seneca, first-century Roman playwright and politician."

"Oh."

Vince had heard of Seneca, but that was all. Here he was supposed to be the English teacher, and this shop teacher-football coach was giving him a lesson in classical literature.

"What about him?"

"Well, he claimed to be a Stoic. That is how history remembers him, in fact. Seneca, the great Roman Stoic. But when he wrote personal letters to his closest friend, he always included an appropriate quotation from Epicurus. The great Stoic quoting the wisdom of Epicurus. So you know what I think? I think he really wanted to be an Epicurean and didn't have courage enough to admit it. Now that is cowardice. I've dreamed about this. If I had the reputation of being someone really bright like Einstein or Bud Wilkinson, I would go around the country making speeches telling everybody the truth about Seneca, setting the record straight."

"You have a cruel streak in you." Vince intentionally lightened the conversation.

Rose welcomed the change in pace. "Yeah. That's why I am a football coach."

"The two go hand in hand, eh?"

"That's the rumor." They both laughed as they imaged the stereotype, and each quietly rejoiced in the thought that at least he was different.

But Vince wasn't through. "OK, but I have a question for you. How do guys like Seneca get this kind of reputation in the first place? They must earn it."

"Not really. People don't really see the person. They just see the position. They know what kind of person they want in that position, so that is what they think."

"It's all in the eye of the beholder then, all make-believe and perception?"

"That's my point. It all starts out that way. But then some guys, most I would imagine, decide—no, that's the wrong word, they don't really decide—they just kind of get railroaded into believing that if that is what people think they are, then that must be the way it is, so they do their best to live up to those perceptions."

"That's a little scary, isn't it? We are just the products of what other people think about us?"

"It takes a lot of courage to live the truth."

As usual, Coach Rose had made his point. He might have started with an end-around move, but he had brought it right back into the middle. As Vince lay quietly trying to figure how to get the conversation into a mood of confession, sweat droplets ran gently down the crevices of his cheeks and worked their way into the corners of his mouth so that he not only felt the intensity of the moment but also tasted it.

"Coach," the tug inside him wanted to carry this opportunity to the point of completion, yet on the surface and at the moment, he hoped Rose was too far into sleep to respond.

"Yes?" The voice was calm, strong, and assuring.

"Do you think I have what it takes to be a courageous man?"

"I don't know, Vincent. I have been too busy thinking about myself, since that answer I made up, to think about anybody else."

"What do you mean?"

"You know what I would really like?"

"What?"

"To be accepted in Wheatheart."

"What do you mean?"

"I would like to be part of the in-crowd."

Lying there in the darkness with sound and legend as the only forms of communication, Vince couldn't take that answer seriously, not at face value. Surely the coach was kidding him, putting him on, maybe even testing him. He wasn't really that shocked by the statement itself. In comfortable moments between two friends, there aren't as many limits or taboos to the flow of expression as there are even when you are alone. So maybe Rose was just thinking aloud, but Vince had to help him. He spoke with a sincerity in his voice which treated the coach's statement as accurate. "I still don't know what you mean."

Coach Rose used the silence which followed to plan an indirect route to the truth, or at least to his own personal perception of it. "Vincent, do you feel like you really belong at Wheatheart, that you are a part of whatever it is the community stands for?"

Vince based his answer on a fleeting glimpse of football, but he camouflaged that image hoping the coach wouldn't know.

"Not really."

"Why not?" Rose's question was bold, demanding a thoughtful and revealing answer.

Vince complied as honestly as he knew how, considering the question and the questioner. "Well, Coach, that's what I was trying to ask about with that business of courage. I always feel like I am a spectator sitting in the bleachers and I don't have the courage to get into the game. You tell me. What's it take to get into the game?"

Rose, the man and not the legend, answered softly, "I don't know, either." He followed his statement with a pregnant silence which assured Vince that he wasn't finished. "Sometimes, most of the time, I don't even know what the game is. I just want to play." Another meaningful silence crept through the darkness as Vince waited, hoping for clarification. "Vincent," he continued obligingly, "I just think I would rather be talked *to* than *about*." With that, he rolled over, as if to say, "Enough of this conversation. I am going to sleep now."

But Vince didn't go to sleep, not for a long time that evening. He lay there in a silence and a darkness filled with the noises and lights of a strange, artificial world and tried to make meaning out of paradoxes.

All during his growing, in that process when he changed from a boy into a man, when he stopped believing because someone told him to and started believing in what he had picked himself, during that growing, regardless of how far he might have shot away from his roots, he still remembered to pray for the abundant life. God had promised it. It was there in the Scripture. That was why Christ came. And since God had promised this life fulfilled, all Vince had to do was ask and expect. And now, after all that asking and expecting, his one model in this race for abundance had come up lame. And suddenly Vince became afraid that maybe God had already given him what he had asked for, and he wasn't smart enough to know it. Maybe that was what Coach Rose meant when he talked about courage. But Vince couldn't ask him. Not now. Not the way he was feeling. But he knew that he couldn't really get close to the coach again until he understood.

With that, Vince went to sleep with his dilemma and lived with it buried just beneath that line which separates conscious from subconscious.

Summer turned to fall and planting. Fall turned to winter. Winter turned to spring and harvest. Spring turned to summer. And summer turned to fall again. And too soon, it was 1980 and Vince was forty-six, sitting in his office waiting for the end of a dismal, windy day and still wondering how to get into a game he still didn't understand.

And worst of all, he still had not met anyone he could ask, "What difference does it make?"

Banking on Intuition
1980

Vince's day at school had been neither full nor fulfilling. It had only been tiring, and he was glad that it was over, although he wasn't really sure why. When you are forty-six, your evenings promise alternatives; but most of the time, even those are routine. Nevertheless, he was happy to get home to hearth and wife.

Professionally, Beth Ann had done well in Wheatheart, and Vince was proud of her. Starting as a teller in 1958, she had become president of Farmer's State Bank five years ago. Hers was a position of honor and power for anybody, and particularly for a woman, in this country where the weather and the nature of much of the work tend to champion natural sex differences. But she had earned her spot. No one had given her anything. Hard work, efficiency, and total commitment were valued traits in Wheatheart, and those in charge of things found some way to reward them. Beth Ann got her chance by being in the right place, but she got her position by earning it.

Of course, her job did alter the family routines a bit. As a principal, Vince had more flexibility and free time, so he took on a larger share of the household chores. Since Beth Ann was schooled in money matters and since she made a higher salary—more than twice as much as Vince—she handled the finances and supervised the buying. Between them, they had moved up into the social caste of comfort. Theirs wasn't the biggest house in Wheatheart, but it did merit a few oohs and aahs when the natives drove by to show out-of-town guests and former students. Although they didn't use the ski boat as much as either would have liked, or said they would have liked, just having it parked on ready beside the drive provided a certain decorative atmosphere to the place. Owning things like that did ease the pain of being forty-six.

Vince had a light supper waiting when Beth Ann got home, about thirty minutes later than he had expected.

Beth Ann was still a handsome woman, not really beautiful but handsome, and Vince always looked forward to seeing her. She was easy to look at, to watch, to study, and after all these years, she still carried a mystique. Vince never really understood how she got to look the way she did. They were always at ease together, but at times he would look at her as if it were the first time he had ever seen her or, even worse, as if he were another wheat farmer trying to borrow the price of this year's steers. She wore her hair short and the color mocked her age. She wore her makeup so discreetly that Vince felt that he was privy to the village secret on the rare occasions when he caught a glimpse of her putting it on. Her stature was trim. Through Vince's inadequacies, she had missed the joys of childbirth and had escaped accumulating those little marks that even the most careful women inherit in the process of motherhood. She was indeed a handsome woman, and when she was occasionally late, Vince had to hide his impatience. He enjoyed seeing her that much.

Actually, Beth Ann's day could have been as distressing as Vince's, except that she wouldn't let it. Since she was in charge, she could control such things. After five years as chief officer at the bank, she was presently battling the first real challenge to her authority, to her decision-making ability, to herself as a person.

Since Wheatheart was a farm community with a farm economy and a farm way of doing business, it just made good sense that the bank should be a farm bank. Oh, it was all right to issue a few car loans, and help the merchants, even the transient ones, redecorate the store fronts and increase the supply of stock during the wet years when harvest promised to be abundant. But mostly, Beth Ann and her bank, the workers and the officers, spent their time helping farmers, lending money on such collateral as cattle and tractors and combines and soil—good red, slightly sandy soil with the capability of nurturing a dying wheat seed into an infant plant and then into a full-grown golden stalk, yielding a hundredfold what was planted. This was the process, the annual process, which made Wheatheart distinctive; and it was this process which Beth Ann worked hard to know and appreciate. With the power of position, she could help that process along, lending a few dollars to this farmer to reseed and renew hopes after last year's crop had been burned by a too hot early wind; financing a land deal so a successful farmer could acquire even more land and success; counseling a cautious farmer in a choice to repair the old tractor or buy a new one; advising customers about such things as investment plans and tax shelters.

This is how Beth Ann had defined her position, and she was good at it. Through years of study, she had made herself a good farm banker. She had driven out to the farms and counted the cattle. She had sifted the soil through her fingers so she could know which was rich and which wasn't. She had learned the names and sizes of tractors so she could recommend the right machine for the job. Through determination and study, she knew the current value of a bushel of wheat and a pound of beef and an acre of land.

For all her hard work, the farmers paid her back with respect. They knew that she knew the business of farming. She didn't know it like they did, with dirt under her fingernails; but with distance, maybe she knew some things even better. At least, they knew that she would never let them get in over their heads with debts they couldn't manage; and the farmers and, subsequently, the whole community respected her as their banker.

But the real world never stays one-dimensional, not the modern world. In spite of how simple or isolated a community may want to keep itself through its success or pride, complexities creep in. And sure enough, the oil industry had come to Wheatheart. It hadn't actually arrived there yet, but it had come to the nearby neighborhoods, close enough to carry the message of a new reality coming into the community.

Some of the oil company representatives had already been in town and bargained with the farmers for drilling rights; to aid them with their bargaining, they had brought big dollars. With this new source of harvest windfall, the farmers had managed to pay off some debts and invest a bit. This brought an economic optimism to the community and, at least temporarily, minimized the importance of wheat prices and rain.

But now the drillers wanted to move in, set up their rigs and equipment, push back the fertile soil to build ponds for the salt water waste, and punch holes deep into the ground hoping to strike a vein of that heavy black liquid which would make the whole enterprise profitable. And they wanted to do it all with a sense of great urgency, as if they had to find that fossil fuel before it mysteriously disappeared, after being buried beneath the Oklahoma earth for thousands of years.

To help them in their urgent quest, the drillers recruited the locals, farmers and entrepreneurs, to assist them with the tangential tasks—building the roads to the well sites, moving the pipe, pushing the dirt back, hauling the equipment and the waste materials. But in order to do this, the locals had to have their own equipment, heavy duty, expensive oil field equipment with not much value to farmers.

So now, Beth Ann's customers and friends expected her to finance their new whims. They came to her with dreams of big money, maybe even wealth, and casually asked for bigger loans than they had ever made in their lives. Pleasantly, Beth Ann stood resolute. One by one, she refused them all. Over the protests, the accusations, the underhanded threats, the calls from the bank directors and her own lending banks, she stood firm, at least on the outside.

She stood firm, but she didn't know why. How could she tell

someone that it was intuition, a sixth sense, that she just didn't feel right about the whole matter? That wasn't enough, not for a business person, a bank president. She had to have a better reason for having her mind.

Maybe she spent so much time learning to be a good farm banker that she didn't want to spend the same time learning to be a good oil field banker, and she couldn't stand the thought of not being good at what she did. Maybe she was old-fashioned, in love with the way things were too much to entertain thoughts of change. Or maybe, because of something in her makeup or her past, she was afraid of the risk and just didn't want to take a chance. Maybe she sensed that there was something immoral here, not in the opportunity but in the desire to take advantage of it. Those people who came to borrow wanted to get rich quick and easy.

Each day, with no clear reason in mind for saying no, and with the stream of oil field opportunists growing thicker, it got harder for Beth Ann to hold firm. But she did, even when she thought she was going to burst from the force outside her pushing against the force inside her. She kept her position, even though she seemed to be the only person in town who felt that way. If anyone else thought like she did, they weren't coming to the bank.

Oh, how she needed a colleague, or a companion, someone who would understand it from her point of view and accept her intuition as reason enough. She had tried to talk about it with Vince, but that was difficult and never very satisfying. She blamed it on Vince, that he was just so nonbusiness-minded that he couldn't understand. But it was more than that and she, at least, knew it. She couldn't talk about bank business with Vince, not comfortably, not honestly, not without guarding what she said to color what she was thinking. He had always seemed interested enough. He had always asked about her work; he had always listened carefully, and he had always been proud of her. She could see that. But still when she talked about the bank, her bank, with her own husband, she felt less of a wife than she wanted to be.

So as she drove home that day to her wifely duties, she took charge of those pent-up feelings inside her, and pushed them below the conversation line.

It was an unusual evening. Neither of them had any place to go, no ball games or play practices or band concerts or town councils or water board or bank meetings, so they took their time with supper and conversation.

Beth Ann opened with a sweeping but cordial line which communicated the face she had put on after she had left the bank, "How did your day go?"

Vince wanted to answer honestly and bluntly. He wanted to shout. He wanted to cry out. "It went like every other day for the past nine years. It went like every day of the world goes." That is what he wanted to say, but he didn't even allow himself to think of it, not even with his own wife. She wouldn't understand. Such an answer would only make him the culprit. So he answered the question and the rest of the evening's conversation the way any forty-six-year-old high school principal and husband of the town banker ought to answer. "It went pretty well. We had a fight."

"Oh, no, football players?" That wasn't just a lucky guess, since every male in Wheatheart High School played football except for three, and they weren't the fighting kind.

"Bobby and Craig." First names were sufficient. As Vince's wife, Beth Ann knew the names of all the students. As president of the bank, she knew their parents, their birthdays, their heritage, and their community contributions and childish pranks. That was also a part of what bankers and merchants and other Wheatheart VIPs did as part of their professional service.

"Did you take care of it to everyone's satisfaction?"

"Yeah. I turned it over to Coach. He will make them run or something."

"Did they have a serious problem?"

"Maybe it is just the time of year. Did you ever feel like slugging someone in November?"

His question pricked her like a thorn on a goathead vine, almost puncturing the facade to let the truth leak out. But she couldn't do that, not tonight when Vince was in this mood.

"It doesn't matter that I feel like it. Civilized people don't go around slugging each other. There are more sophisticated methods for handling reactions. Isn't that what you all are teaching in school?"

Vince couldn't tell whether that was a wifely chide or a community challenge, so he decided to take it good-naturedly. There wasn't any reason to make issues when none existed. But the official part of Beth Ann couldn't drop the fight topic until she had more information. She had to know a reason for the fight. Tomorrow morning she had to be as knowledgeable as her customers would be. Her position in the community demanded that. Besides, her information would be official because it would be the principal's report, a cut above the idle gossip of the Dew Drop Inn or John Deere place.

"But what touched them off today, anything important?"

"Molly Sue, I think."

"Well, I would say she's important. Is Craig interested?"

"I don't know and I am not sure he knows. When they are that age, I doubt that any of them know what they want. Just get through today and have as much fun as you can because somehow tomorrow is going to take care of itself when it gets here, and all your dreams are going to come true."

Beth Ann shuddered inside as she thought of the similarities between her world and Vince's. She wanted to shudder outside too, but she couldn't. That wasn't what her husband needed just then.

"That's a rather harsh commentary on the youth of America. I have never heard you talk that way before."

"I don't think I have ever felt this way before."

"Vince, you're getting old." She laughed as she said it, and Vince knew she meant it as a passing joke, a figure of speech, a transition from this topic to something lighter, but he didn't appreciate it at this moment anyhow. Maybe it was too close to what he had been feeling all day long himself. So he tried to release the pain with plans.

"Beth Ann, let's spend the weekend in the City." It was more than a spur-of-the-moment thought. He had had it in the back of his mind as a suitable prescription to cure his feelings.

"What?"

"Let's spend the whole weekend in the City. We get out of school Friday at 12:03." (Only the principal would know the exact time.) "We could run over for the ball game and stay Friday night and Saturday night. Maybe go to one of those hotels with an indoor pool and just swim and relax and forget that winter is coming."

This was an appeal from an unhappy husband, but for her it was more than that. It was an offer, a chance to escape. Both wife and banker loved the invitation, but she knew she couldn't accept. She hated telling Vince the reason.

"But what if the team wins? You will need to be home for the celebration."

"Let Casteel handle it. In the nine years I have been principal, we have won the state in football four times. This town could do a state championship victory celebration in its sleep. By now everybody knows his role by heart. No one would ever miss me. I could stand in the middle of the whole affair stark naked and no one would ever notice. They are just going through the routine."

"That may be so, but if you weren't there, the whole town would make gossip fodder out of your absence for months."

"Let them. They've got to gossip about something. It may as well be us. In fact, it might even be exciting for a change."

She agreed, but only beneath the conversation line. "Maybe for you, but not for me. I just can't afford the price. Not now. Besides, Vince, I can't even go to the game."

Although their relationship really didn't demand a soft spot to drop that bomb, she at least sought out the right moment, somewhere in the conversation where Vince was already cushioned for the blow. As usual, her timing was well directed.

"What?" Vince tried to sound shocked, although he wasn't really. He had come to expect such surprises, but he thought that if he could sound shocked, it would cover up the anger in his voice.

"Bank examiners." Since the answer was more than common, it

didn't need any elaboration. These people always seemed to come at the wrong time.

"What?" The shock was wearing thin in places and the anger was beginning to seep through.

"What else? You know how important it is for me to go to the game. Why else would I miss it?"

"But not this week!"

"They invite themselves. I don't invite them."

"But not this week!"

She agreed both in thought and feeling. But one of them had to stay calm, to understand, so that was her job just now. "I didn't have any choice, Vince. You can go to the game with some of the men. It will give you a chance to be with your friends without the intrusion of female interference. What do we know about football anyway? You will have a better time if I'm not there."

Vince resented her attempt to placate him, but he checked his anger sufficiently to form a defensive remark. "All the other guys are going with their wives."

She refused to let him score the point. "Maybe their wives don't have to be examined."

Sensing her uneasiness, he softened the tone. "Well, I have examined my wife and found her pretty terrific. I don't see why these other men have to do it too."

She welcomed the new direction. It gave her a chance to be a wife again. "Why, Vince Benalli, that sounds like a young man talking."

"Come spend the weekend with me and I will show you young."

"I wish I could. You know that. But have a good time anyway." Although the conversation ended on a compatible note, the following silence, filled with insignificant cleaning chores, was slightly tense. Beth Ann wrapped herself in her banker's voice and changed the topic. "Vince, I was thinking that maybe you ought to trade your car in this month or next. The new models should be out in a week or so and you do need to trade."

"Has it been two years already? I really hadn't thought about it."

"How would you like a new Firebird?"

"What?"

"You know. That jazzy little sports car Pontiac has. It is actually a pretty good buy when you think of the resale. What do you think?" This all came from the banker's side of the conversation. Something inside told her this was a good decision.

Vince stood tall and assumed an air of authority. "Lady, I am the high school principal," and he wanted to go on. He wanted to say, "I am forty-six years old." But he caught himself and mockingly hid behind the position and left the age unsaid.

"Maybe it would change your image and you wouldn't be so grumpy." The wife laughed as if she was apologizing for the unpleasantness she had created with her weekend responsibility.

Vince decided to cooperate with her, to make things lighter. "Why, what have you heard?"

She played along. "Oh, you know how the talk goes. 'Old Man Benalli is getting crotchety in his old age. The way things are going, he may call off Christmas this year.' "

By this time, each on his own had agreed to stem the tension and avoid expressing the mutual hurts which had been bubbling beneath the surface all evening, and they came to bed with feigned good spirits and a too easy laughter.

Almost by habit, Vince finished his daily ritual by emptying the contents of his pockets. Yesterday's announcement sheet folded four times with words written in red was casually tossed into an almost full dresser drawer, one of the smaller ones of course, which had been designated for this purpose years ago. Having completed that duty, he rummaged through an expensive leather-bound copy of *Spoon River Anthology* which he kept on the nightstand for times such as this. Somewhere in this collection of small-town epitaphs, he usually could find the right expression for the way he was feeling or wanted to feel when he woke up tomorrow, looking forward to another day at Wheatheart High. Wheatheart, or Spoon River, or Gotebo, or Potato City, it really didn't make a lot of difference. Masters had uncovered small-townness and bunched it into words so that when Vince read, he could think, "I wish I had said that."

But on the Monday night before the state championship football game, Vince was just flipping restlessly through the pages. He couldn't find meaning in the right words, probably because he was looking for the answer to a specific question. But he already knew the answer to the question, and he knew that he knew, and he knew that he was the only person who knew. Not Masters, not Casteel, with all his confidence, and not even Rose. Vince knew the answer, but he didn't want to admit it because it was another part of what it meant to be forty-six. But he still wanted to ask the question— "Why did he have to go to the ball game alone?"

On the other side of the bed, Beth Ann pushed the day and the night out of her mind and fell asleep quickly. Neither of them remembered a night somewhere in the spring of 1958 when this all started.

You Can Never Go Back
1958

"The bank called again today, Vince." Beth Ann had waited all evening for the right moment for that announcement, if there ever is a right time. As usual, Vince had come home from school with papers to grade, lessons to prepare, and thoughts and stories to tell. With all the things which Vince did, he could do them better when he felt good about himself. He just didn't need bad news in the middle of the evening. Now that they were in bed, and he was finished for the day, she decided to risk it.

"Oh, no, that's not what I wanted to hear." Vince tried to hide a whole wave of emotions, but he wasn't good at it.

"Same old thing. What should they do with our checks for the next ten days until you get paid?" One of the advantages of teaching in a small town was that the bank honored all the checks, even the overdrafts. It was a kind of loan arrangement between the bank and the teachers.

"Well, you ought to be getting pretty friendly with those people. They call every month." He tried to tease her.

"What are we going to do, Vince? Will there ever be enough money?"

"I don't know. A year ago when we were in college, we thought we would be in tall cotton if we ever made this much money, and now look at us. The car is gone. The refrigerator is so old it looks like something out of the wreck of the Hesperus. And this place is sure no mansion fit for a king or even a basketball coach, for that matter. Where does it go? Why can't we have things?" He wasn't asking her. He was asking the world, or whatever powers run it.

"Well, maybe it isn't important that we have any more—if we just had the money to pay for what we already have." She tried to sound encouraging.

"Well, it is important. It just seems to me that we ought to be able to live better than this. We are professional people. We are entitled to more."

He was upset and she needed to help him. "We still have each other, and we have a lot of fun."

"Come on, Beth Ann. Be serious. This just isn't fair. Look at the time it takes. It isn't like I could run out and get a part-time job. Five nights out this week. Six nights out last week. Lesson preparations every night."

Sometimes Vince missed the bright side. "Yes, but isn't it fun? We do get to spend a lot of time together."

"I agree. It is a great life, but we just have to have more money. We can't go on living like this, from month to month. I almost said 'from mouth to mouth.' What is that expression? Hand to mouth!" They both giggled at his slip. It wasn't all that funny, but maybe the reason for it was.

"I would be happy if we just had enough in our hand to last the whole month!"

"That is what I mean. We get this call from the bank today. We have ten days left this month that we can't buy one single thing. We can't even make a contribution to the church. And now I am going to spend the next ten days being totally unhappy every time I think about it. Presto, the check comes, and twenty days later we start all over again."

"But it will get better, Vince. It will get better," she said as encouragingly as she knew how.

"I keep telling myself that too, but I am not sure. I am really not convinced. We have got to do something different, and we sure can't save anywhere else. We have cut so many corners now I am getting dizzy."

She thought about that for a while, and then changed the tone. "I don't know. I think I have been rather creative with hamburger and macaroni."

"You know what I mean, Beth Ann. We can't live this way. It just ain't fittin' for a coach."

"So what do you suggest, Coach? I don't see you giving up your profession." That was a risky thing to say. She didn't even want to plant the thought in his mind. But she wanted to help him evaluate.

"That's the point. I am not going to give it up. I can't, Beth Ann. You've got to understand that." Again, he wasn't just trying to convince Beth Ann. He was trying to convince those thousands of people not in the room who didn't understand why talented, bright college graduates teach.

"I do understand." She was sincere, even beyond what being his wife would have demanded.

"Even if no one else will say it, I will. Doggone it, I'm good. Do you know how many lousy teachers there are in this world? No wonder kids are turned off to school. We've got those teachers and you know who they are. They just go through the motions. They act as if they don't even like kids. They don't give a thing of themselves." He could have gone on, but she had heard it all before.

"Well, no one can say that about my Vince Benalli. He gives of himself. That's for sure."

Caught up in his own anger, he missed her tone. "Are you criticizing?"

Her retort carried the force of sincerity. "You know better than that, Vince. I am so proud of you. Just today, Bobby Walker's mother stopped me and said that for the first time her son enjoys English. Here you have been at Wheatheart less than a year and already you have those kids turned on to English."

He calmed into a happier image. "They really are catching on. I really think I can see a difference. I watch the books they bring into class, what they check out of the library, and I am beginning to see some good stuff. I really believe this work is paying off. And look at the basketball team. We didn't win the regional like football, but it was the best season they have had in ten years."

"I am proud of you, Vince." She was half sincere and half flirty.

"I just wish it didn't take so much time, or paid more."

"Does it have to take all that time?" It was a simple question without any hidden meaning.

"It does, Beth Ann, it does. These kids need somebody they can talk to, somebody they can reach; and to do that, you just have to be around. I guess there are easier ways. Take that paper grading. Rader said to me yesterday, 'If you didn't assign all those papers, you wouldn't have to read them.' But how else will kids learn to write? And if I don't teach them to write, I have cheated them. I really believe that." It helped him to say these things to her. He was clarifying it for himself at the same time.

"You have convinced me, Vince. So I just talk to the nice lady at the bank every month."

"But that's not right, either. It just seems to me that we are entitled to have a car that will at least get us somewhere."

"If we had the money to go," Beth Ann added quickly.

"Yes, as much as I love this place, or at least like what I am doing, I would like to get away once in a while, and we just don't have the money." They both paused and remembered family picnics and pleasant trips.

When she thought about it in years to come, Beth Ann realized that she should have let the conversation die there. Vince was still unhappy, too unhappy to think about his teaching or his students, and that wasn't fair to him. She tried the lightest thing she could think of. "Maybe I will write a cookbook, *101 Ways to Disguise Hamburger So that Your Husband Will Think You Are a Wonderful Cook*. What do you think of the title?"

"A bit long to be catchy. But I might have a suggestion."

Now she was afraid of what she had done. "I am not sure I like that tone of voice, Vince. You are just beginning to sound serious."

"Okay, maybe I am a little serious; but have you thought of going to work?"

"No." Her answer was convincingly terse, even if it wasn't quite true.

"Oh, now I *know* you have thought about it. Half the women in Wheatheart work and those farmers' wives work all the time. They just don't leave home to do it." Universality made it sound like it wasn't a really big deal, like he was a little boy trying to steal her first kiss.

But this universality didn't apply to her. "OK, so I thought about it. Maybe once in a while when that nice woman calls from the bank. But Vince, I don't want to go to work."

He waited until the flush had ebbed. And then he said, almost pleadingly, "We've got to have more money."

"I know that being without money is tough; it's tough on both of us, but it has to be really tough on you." She paused to convince him that she understood. "And I am not lazy, Vince." Again she paused to give herself time to change directions. "I do work, but my having a job will change things." She said that as matter-of-factly as she knew how, but it still carried the shrillness of fear.

Vince must have detected the fear because he tried to sound reassuring but forceful. "I know that. I have thought about that, and I am willing to make the sacrifice. After all, it's only temporary until we get past those first couple of years when they really take advantage of new teachers."

She hurried a reply, but it was something she had thought about. "No, it isn't. It is never temporary. We may think so, but once you change things, change a relationship, you can never go back to where it was before."

Vince used the stillness to formulate a response—one which would convince both of them. "I am not sure that's biblical. Isn't that the meaning of being saved? You are forgiven. You can start all over again. Brand new."

She protested the change in direction as much as the analogy. "Now, Vince, you know I can't get philosophical with you, but I know one thing—if one of your students gives up her virginity, she may be forgiven for it, but she will still never be a virgin again."

"But that doesn't have anything to do with us. We love each other. We have a temporary need. We meet it with a temporary method. That's all there is to it." He made it sound as if she were off the point.

The silence crept between them and built a small chasm, one which he couldn't jump over. Perhaps he didn't see the need because he had spoken last, and husbands should have the last word.

"Vince?" Her voice disturbed the darkness.

"Yes?" He wanted the conversation to go on, but he was afraid of it too.

"I don't think I am selfish." She was a little girl again, looking for affirmation.

"You are not selfish. I never said you were." He was defensive.

"Those things I do—going to all the ball games and sitting with the parents, it is so funny. At times I get the idea that some mother is about ready to say something really nasty about you and then she sees me and stops right in mid-sentence. And that women's club at church—I ask myself why I go. They are all mothers and we just sit around and pass the babies back and forth, but I feel like we are getting into the spirit of the community. And the people in the stores take time to talk and be friendly. Vince, aren't those things important?" She was still trying to get past the defense.

"They are very important." He said it with some pain.

"And just being with you, Vince, and knowing what you do. I know you are the best teacher up there, and I don't just have to take your word for it. I have seen what you do. I see you around the students. I get to go to the ball games. Vince, I don't want to give all that up. I just want us to go on being like we are." She might have been pleading, but she was honest.

"And we will go on just like we are. Your going to work won't change anything. It's just temporary. I'll help with the house."

Although he had not detected a change in the tone, he took charge again.

"Vince, it's more than housecleaning. It's the reason I want to clean the house that I don't want to lose." She pleaded innocently.

"It's just for now. We won't lose anything." Dutifully he reassured her.

She paused as if to question herself and to question him as well. "How can I know that?"

"Don't be silly. You just know. That is the way we are. That is the way things are." He was both husband and father.

But it wasn't just a matter of his authority. "I'm not trying to be silly and I am trying not to be selfish. I just want to make sure we have thought about this before we do it."

"Now are you accusing me of not being able to think through things?" He was almost pouting.

Like a mother, she took charge. "I am not accusing you of anything. And you don't need to get so defensive. If your mind is so made up, if you have already decided what's best for us, if you are so sure, I'll find a job. I just want you to know where it might lead." That was more than a threat. It was also a warning.

After the silence had chipped away at the ice, Vince tried the warmth of charm. "I know where it is going to lead. We are going to have a little money left over for the last ten days of the month, and you won't have to talk to that nice woman at the bank anymore."

He could tell she was angry. "That's where you are wrong, Buddy-Buddy, because that is exactly where I am going to go get a job."

In their life together—three years of dating and since their marriage before their senior year of college—he had never seen her that way before. He had struck something sensitive, and he tried to pull away. But he didn't know which direction to take. He tried teasing. "Aw, come on. What do you know about banking?"

"I don't know anything, but I can learn. I'll show you." By now, she didn't sound angry anymore, but she did sound determined.

And she did learn. She learned faster than anyone could have believed. Maybe she was motivated by a strong force. But whatever the reason, she learned enough that by 1980 she was the bank president who had to refuse oil field borrowers and meet with the bank examiners who came to town on the weekend of the state championship football game.

More than a Meal

1980

In Wheatheart, breakfast was more than a meal. It was the social hour, the newscast, and the community commentary all rolled into one. As its rightful community service, the Dew Drop Inn opened for business at five o'clock and served breakfast until the bacon and eggs customers merged into the coffee and ice tea group, as morning wore into day and the world steadied itself with forenoon tedium.

Vince was part of the middle breakfast club, coming about 6:30 for an hour of food and talk before he had to get to school.

He rarely took Beth Ann with him. Breakfast at the Dew Drop was a male event, like a backwoods cockfight; and having a woman present, except, of course, Rosemary the waitress, who was as tough as any man in town anyway, drastically altered the quality of the verbal interaction and accompanying gestures. As president of the bank, Beth Ann was more than a mere woman, a farmer's wife, or even a merchant's wife who clerked in her husband's store. Her position entitled her to a certain amount of perspective which made her comments on such items as wheat prices, the lack of rain, and the football team more acceptable than other women's ideas would have been. But she was still a woman.

This morning, Vince went alone. He had asked her. He always asked. But she didn't want to go. She didn't give any reasons; maybe she didn't know the reasons. But secretly, where he didn't want to admit it, Vince was glad. Yesterday had been so full with being forty-six that he wanted to forget the walls in front of him built out of the material of the walls behind him. He was searching for promise or escape, he didn't know which; besides, the two looked so much alike that he wasn't interested in seeing the difference.

Today, the weather was as docile as yesterday had been turbulent. The sun came up clear across the eastern sky and turned the hills behind it purple. The silt and sand from yesterday's winds lay undisturbed at the edges of the streets and in the corners of the fences and flower beds. The only breeze was a gentle one which caressed the face and promised a touch of warmth before noon. On the open prairie, fall days can be either nasty or memorable, and this one was definitely worth remembering. It promised to be the kind of day which made living worthwhile, even if there weren't any promises left.

As usual, weather was a feature topic of the Dew Drop Inn early morning report. In farm country, the weather is more than a scientific phenomenon. It is an industrial partner—fate or God's will. It not only chooses your activities and directs your timing, but it determines your success. The good farmers, those who produce enough every year to stay ahead of their bank loans and maybe even buy something new, got good by guessing. Every farmer weighs the evidence and then guesses—when it will rain and how much, how the winds will blow, and what the hot gusts of September really mean this year. But some, either by luck or skill or holy favor, guess right more often than the others, and they are the good farmers. And on those years when they and the weather work together instead of against each other, they make more money, and they spend more money, and the merchants and bankers smile and talk about the weather during breakfast.

By the time Vince got to the Dew Drop Inn Cafe on the west side of Main Street, halfway between the high school at one end and the John Deere equipment yards at the other end, the town was already well represented. First, there was Scott Garland, junior partner in the John Deere store who with his father, Art, kept the Wheatheart area farmers supplied with tractors, combines, wheatdrills, time payments, and up-to-date community news. Although Scott had been an active student about the time Vince first came to Wheatheart, and had received ultimate distinction—all-state football player—and had done well in community affairs and was always pleasant, sometimes there was a note of bitterness in his tone. He always seemed to remember his days in sports rather than his days in class. Vince also noticed that when the breakfast chatter turned to praise of Coach Rose, as it often did, Scott took that time to eat a few bites of his breakfast; and for that reason, Vince never knew for sure whether that young business tycoon could be trusted.

Moss Bosco, local artist, sat on a stool and sipped slowly from a cup of hot tea, the only one Rosemary would serve all day. Every community is entitled to one eccentric, and Moss was Wheatheart's very own. He served the role well, better than some other area eccentrics. Moss was actually bright and quite harmless. In fact, he seemed almost normal, if one could forget about that flowing white beard and that little French cap which held his full head of white hair in check. By night he kept to himself mostly, showing up once in a while at a basketball game, but never at a football game. But during the day, he was visible, more than visible, conspicuous, ubiquitous. He was everywhere. He painted signs and helped wallpaper houses. He designed company logos, and created and painted the Whippet emblem in the middle of the basketball court at the gym. This week he was particularly busy because several merchants had commissioned him to mark their storefronts with sincere congratulatory and motivational football comments. So Moss was as much into the spirit of the week as the rest of the community, but he wouldn't be at the game.

There were also the usual farmers—Lyman Smith, Reinschmidt,

Kellar, Jantzen—who provided Wheatheart with the crops and the kids which made the town prosperous, both at the bank and at the school. Actually, the farmers in for breakfast this early were not just plain farmers; they were the agribusinessmen who had the collateral to borrow more and operate bigger than their neighbors. Since they were businessmen, they could come into town for breakfast, coffee, and news, rather than performing the mundane chores which owners of simpler farms had to do.

The mercantile industry was represented by such people as Ed Rogers who ran the Culligan Soft Water store and a few other sidelines. Though he was a native of Wheatheart and high school graduate of several years back, he didn't act much like it. He had fathered three daughters but not a son, so he was not the least bit interested in football, and that quirk marked him as something of an outsider, or at best a rather strange native. Carl Bledsoe was there too. Carl had come to Wheatheart a few years ago when he had retired from the navy and had set up a small book and gift store in one of the frequently vacant storefronts on Main Street. He was a friendly fellow and so actively involved in community affairs that he seemed to be making a go of a business which really shouldn't have had much of a chance in Wheatheart. The locals, both the natives and the newcomers, shopped merchants rather than stores, and his success proved the value of friendliness.

An unusual entry in that farm group this morning was Abe Ericson, Jimmy Charles' father. Abe didn't have breakfast in town all that regularly. He was mostly a home person who farmed well and independently. As part of the old, traditional Wheatheart stock, Abe was one of the few farmers who still kept a butcher calf and milked a cow. It wasn't really a matter of economics. He could afford to buy milk like everyone else in modern Wheatheart, but somehow chores were a part of his code, a part of his legend.

Since he was in town this morning, he had to have had a special reason. Since he was a person inside himself who never really talked much in these sessions, Vince would never know what it was. He could only guess.

This was the week of the state championship, and Abe was a real fan. Or perhaps he had already heard about the fight and wondered if Bobby's punishment would be just enough to make a place for his son in that important game.

But surely, Vince reasoned, Abe knew his own son well enough to know that Jimmy Charles would rather know how people become poets than play football. Surely Abe knew that and found delight in the son he had raised. But maybe he didn't.

Brother Bob, the Baptist preacher, was another unusual breakfast eater that morning. But for him, nothing was out of the ordinary. He had a flexible schedule which he used to achieve the unexpected. He went where he could meet people, shake hands, and generally be friendly and encouraging. But he still managed the time to tend to such ministerial duties as comforting the bereaved, visiting the sick, and preaching the sermon twice every Sunday and once on Wednesday night.

In his more than twenty-five years at Wheatheart, Brother Bob had actually grown up in the ministry, but no one noticed it because the community couldn't remember any difference. He had always fulfilled the image of what a preacher is supposed to be. Next to Coach Rose, Brother Bob was the most talked-about man in town. The difference between them was that Brother Bob sometimes showed up in crowds, such as at Dew Drop Inn at breakfast. He never really contributed that much to the conversation beyond the greetings, but he did affect it. Although the complaints were just as sharp, the language was purer and the jokes cleaner.

Earl Bresserman, the new young policeman was sitting beside Moss, having his last cup of coffee before he retired from his night rounds and went home for a few hours of sleep. Earl was new to Wheatheart. He had come in about a year before from somewhere over east, when the town council decided that Wheatheart needed more police protection than what old Mr. Baker could provide anymore. Old Mr. Baker had been the town constable as long as anyone could remember. He got up every day at four in the afternoon and spent his time until midnight riding around in the old black and white car the town bought for him, stopping to check the doors of every store to make sure nothing had been left insecure for the evening.

But the town council decided that in these modern days of rampant immorality, the community needed more modern police methods; so they bought a new car, retired old Mr. Baker, and brought in Earl who had been trained in some middle-sized police department. Sure enough, just as they expected, crime increased; Earl was kept busy and appeared even busier than he was; and old Mr. Baker quietly died three months later. By then, he had been out of the limelight long enough that only a handful could find the time to make it to his funeral.

Of course, Charlie Brady was at the Dew Drop Inn. Charlie was almost anywhere there was a crowd, and he had a story for every occasion. It didn't matter much that he really didn't have that many stories. He could tell the same one over and over again without any trouble, just as long as he remembered it clearly enough to maintain some consistency in the plot line.

Others, merchants and farmers alike, moved in and out through the morning and the conversation.

"Boy, she blowed yesterday!"

"Ain't that the truth. Never saw it so bad this early in November." For the Oklahoma farmers, unless the weather was Edenlike favorable, it was the worst on record—or at least as long as the natives could remember.

"Did it do you any hurt?"

"Well, it didn't do me no good. I can tell you that for sure."

"Well, thank God we got a little moisture, enough to hold the roots in place, if she's going to blow like that much."

"Yeah, but the way she blowed yesterday, it can sure get dry in a hurry, then where we going to hide?"

"Nothing feels good when it blows like that. Why, I think it blew my old steers off feed. They sure didn't eat good this morning." Vince wondered if the rest of the town crowd caught that message—the farmer-businessman had already started his workday.

"Speaking of steers, did I ever tell you boys about the time we had a bunch of old steers get tipsy eating some stale silage?" Charlie Brady had told that story somewhere around town at least once a week for the past forty years, and now he was beginning to believe it himself.

When the story had subsided, Scott Garland changed the tone. "Hey, Earl, what was that bunch of beer bottles broke all over the street up by the hospital?"

Earl's answers always reflected his image of himself as cop. "Well, you can expect some of that kind of thing when the kids are as excited as they are this week."

"Had a bad night?"

"Not really. I was out and ready for them. They know that, and that really cuts down on what they do. Just being around makes a lot of difference. We call that preventive law enforcement. It is sure a lot better than waiting until they raise Cain and tear something up."

"Well, you're sure right, Earl. I don't understand it, but we always seem to get some foolishness on the week of the state championship game," a bystander observed.

"Well, keep a lid on 'em, Earl." They all nodded approval.

"I'm going to do that. You can tell 'em that." The young policeman was confident.

"At least, you've got Rose helping you out."

"He's good help."

"Ain't that the truth!"

"He sure understands kids."

"Best I've ever seen."

"We are sure lucky to have him."

"That should be obvious, come Friday night at Taft Stadium."

"Did you ever see one who knows both football and kids like he does?"

On this topic, everyone in the Dew Drop had his say, everyone except for Vince who only listened and Scott who ate his steak and eggs.

"By the way, has anybody heard what wheat is this morning?"

"Three dollars and four bits, I think."

"That's Kansas City prices."

"Moisture's good. Steers ought to do well."

"Saw old Orley Orris the other day. Lives somewhere up in Colorado."

"Hey, Rosie, did you make this coffee yesterday? Sure is bitter."

"Maybe she strained it through a gunnysack."

"I don't know, it tastes to me like an improvement."

"Bought one small gear and it cost $184."

"That's unions for you."

"If he gets elected again, we're all going to go broke."

"Did you hear about that long-haired hippy who killed his old lady and shot himself?"

"Moisture's good."

"Steers are fat."

"This cup is better than the last one."

"I think we've got a chance."

"Rose always has some trick up his sleeve."

"It just ain't like it used to be."

"Kids just seem to be getting wilder."

"That dope is bad business, I tell you."

"Those old steers just got drunk and laid around and bellered."

"I ain't going with that government program again. I think I can make more money cutting mine."

"Moisture's good, but we are going to need some snow."

"Worst dirt storm in November I can remember."

The conversation ran on from reports to commentaries, and Vince tried to remember how it was different from last year or ten years ago or even twenty years ago, but he couldn't. What would it be like if you ever had something significant to talk about? But maybe at forty-six, there isn't anything significant or even new.

"Hey, Vince!" He was ready for this part. He had been expecting it all morning and when it came, he was relieved. However, he had expected it to come from Scott Garland; instead, Lyman Smith brought it up. "I hear you had a little battle up there yesterday."

"Yeah, Vince, tell us about that." Charlie Brady was interested for another reason. He needed new material for storytime and his grandson's heroics might merit embellishing.

Abe Ericson stared at his coffee cup.

"It wasn't much. They just shouted and shoved mostly." Vince knew the school belonged to the community, all of it, the kids, the accomplishments, and even the embarrassments, and he knew he owed some explanation; but he wasn't always sure why.

"Reckon they may try it again?" Charlie was still after something juicier than what Vince was willing to squeeze out of it.

"No, I don't think so. They are actually pretty good friends. They just had this one small disagreement." In spite of how small it was, and how small Vince made it in his report, the whole incident would grow through the day. It would be good if he could nip it before it bloomed too vividly, not just because it was state championship week, but because he was forty-six years old and just didn't have the spare emotions to honor a major problem.

"Over Molly Sue, I heard." As another indication of his latent bitterness, Scott kept records of the rumors and the undercurrents.

"Oh, really?" Vince evaded, but with a purpose he hoped he could justify. A love triangle, even among high school students, is still more refreshingly scandalous than two football players beating on each other. Somehow such gossip stimulated the imaginations, or maybe dulled the realities of middle age temporarily. Since Vince just couldn't get into that attitude, he didn't want anyone else to enjoy the pleasure either.

"I guess Rose took care of it." Scott's tone did not reflect the optimism which would have come through if someone else had made that statement which all of them were thinking.

Abe Ericson stared at his coffee cup.

"I think he made them run or something." Vince was staying as casual as he could, despite his anger toward the words and the feelings everyone held but nobody stated.

"Well, there will be some more devilment up there this week." One of the farmers was just making conversation.

"Yeah, Vince. Keep a lid on it up there until this is all over." Another farmer offered fatherly advice. He was entitled to do that because he was a farmer and a father, and above that, a football fan who wanted an uneventful state championship performance on Friday evening.

"Keep a lid on it," Vince thought. "Keep a lid on it." And he had a vision of working in a pickle factory where he crammed green monsters into a jar too small and screwed the cap on tight so that nothing would leak out and stain the routine which was one man's glory and another's middle-age boredom.

"Keep a lid on it. Is that all I do?" And to answer the question he was thinking, he remembered a time when he knew for sure.

More Good Days Than Bad
1958

"Walter, would you like to read this poem?"

"Nope." The whole class laughed. They always laughed at Walter's smart remarks. The young teacher didn't understand that. A lot of them didn't like Walter, didn't appreciate his disruptive influence. They thought he was a nuisance, with his country swagger which rejected anything fine that couldn't be bought with money. But they still laughed when he disrupted class and got the best of a teacher, even a teacher they liked as much as Mr. Benalli. Although Vince didn't understand why they laughed, he knew they had to; so he accepted it with the patience which characterized his style.

"Well, do us a favor anyway, Walter. You've got such a melodious voice, and this poem requires a mature, melodious rendering. It should be something right down your alley. You are a pretty mature junior." Mr. Benalli put high expectations on high expectations, and he usually got results.

"You got it, Coacher, if you say so. Here she blows."

"When Richard Cory went downtown . . ."

"Now, Walter, look at that again." Mr. Benalli's interruption was gently encouraging.

"Okay, so it says 'Whenever.' But what difference does that make? When, whenever, it's the same thing."

"Not really." The teacher seized this opportunity to teach his class something profound about the aesthetics of language. He never knew when such a chance might come again. "What is the difference between these two words?"

"I think I know, Mr. Benalli." Marie was always eager to answer his questions, but her enthusiasm for class did not make her the most popular student in school. This time the teacher managed the class reaction with a casual grin which both assured and quieted those who would discourage her.

"Yes, Marie?"

"It has something to do with the rhythm, the meter. Poets use stuff like that to make their poems flow."

"You mean like a song?" The mention of rhythm alerted Billy because he played the bass drum in the marching band.

The smile on the young teacher's face was real, not fake, and the students sensed it. "That's exactly what it is, Billy. Songs are just poems put to music. Let me give you a line of poetry and you tap it out for us so we can hear it.

"The stag at eve had drunk its fill."

From more than obedience, Billy took his pencil and tapped out an iambic beat. "Great," the teacher commended him and consequently, the whole class, because it was evident that they were comprehending. "That is called iambic. Can somebody give me a definition for iambic?"

Walter responded, which was unusual because he generally used classtime to draw football trap plays so he could understand his role as fullback better. "Sounds like a short beat followed by a long beat."

"I am really impressed at how smart you guys are today. Have you been taking smart pills on me again?" Mr. Benalli alluded to a slightly dirty joke. He knew the students knew the joke; but since they didn't know if he knew the joke, they snickered among themselves. "Now, Billy, give me the reverse of that."

Billy tapped a trochaic beat with his pencil on his desk. "What do you think that is called?" the teacher asked optimistically.

Again, Marie was on the spot. "Trochaic."

"Okay, Walter. It's your turn. Give me a definition of trochaic."

"Long and short." Walter had gained a lot of confidence since the discussion had started.

The class had learned something and Mr. Benalli wanted to make it permanent. "I wonder if we can think of something to help us remember those terms, so that when we hear the rhythms in songs we can impress our friends with our new knowledge."

Billy had the sense of rhythm. "How about this. Iambic short and long. Iambic short and long. Trochaic long and short. Trochaic long and short." And with the teacher's hand gesture invitation, the class joined in for their newfound cheer.

As the chant dwindled into oblivion, Walter asked, "Hey, do you reckon this poem here will ever be set to music?"

"Maybe," Mr. Benalli encouraged him. "It sounds like something Simon and Garfunkel might do. Now read for us." And this time, Walter got it letter perfect, and with feeling.

Whenever Richard Cory went downtown,
    We people on the pavement looked at him;
He was a gentleman from sole to crown,
    Clean-favored, and imperially slim.

And he was always quietly arrayed,
    And he was always human when he talked;
But still he fluttered pulses when he said,
    "Good morning," and he glittered when he walked.

And he was rich—yes, richer than a king—
    And admirably schooled in every grace:
In fine, we thought that he was everything
    To make us wish that we were in his place.

So on we worked, and waited for the light,
  And went without the meat, and cursed the bread;
And Richard Cory, one calm summer night,
  Went home and put a bullet through his head.

He finished with a flourish, paused for a pregnant moment and added his commentary. "Hey, that's neat."

The young teacher played disinterested. "What's neat?"

"This poem. I like it." And the rest of the class showed their collective approval, each in his own way.

"Well, what makes it neat?" Of course, he was prompting, employing the Socratic method, as the experts would say; but he was also intrigued. He hadn't been in teaching long enough to know what qualifies a poem to earn the high prize of "neat."

"This is a neat story. They think this guy is Joe Cool and all the time he's been playing too long without a helmet." Euphemisms for strange behavior are frequently local, reflecting the values and color of a specific culture. Thus, the comment was communicative.

"Wait a minute. Who's they?" Mr. Benalli focused the question more generally, to let Walter off the hook. He didn't want to run him out of answers while he still had his confidence up. Roger Wilson, a solid B student, somewhat a fan of poetry and a Wheatheart native, answered for the class.

"That's us."

"What do you mean, that's us?" Mr. Benalli sensed the mental rumblings which shake a classroom just before a good discussion erupts.

"He says it up above." Now everyone was getting some ideas in. "We people on the pavement. That's us."

"Who?"

"Everybody who thinks somebody else is better off."

Mr. Benalli was still young enough in the profession to be surprised at the direction discussions sometimes took. "So you think you feel that way?"

"Sure we do. Maybe everybody does, but we people in

Wheatheart sure do. We watch TV and think, 'Wouldn't it be great to live in California or New York or London or somewhere like that!' "

"So you really think that?"

Another student offered another version of the same answer. "Or we think we would like to be rich or famous."

"So what kind of an attitude is that?"

This time, the answer to the teacher's question lay a little deeper below the surface and required a bit more drilling before it could come to the top, but Mr. Benalli had been in this situation enough to know to wait for the good stuff. He wasn't comfortable with the silence, but he was disciplined enough to tolerate it. Finally, somebody trying to make a connection to Sunday School or something holy said, "Do you call it coveting?"

Mr. Benalli's low profile chuckle was more to hide the fact that he hadn't thought of that than to show amusement. But he went on. "That's a good answer. Maybe that is what it is, but what else could it be?"

"Well, it sure ain't honest." The owner of this answer was a boy named Danny, meek and usually dirty, who lived on the outskirts of town and the outskirts of the crowd. This was the first time he had ever spoken in English class, and he had written even less.

"Why isn't it honest?" There could be no mistaking the direction of that question. Danny was caught up, whether he wanted to be or not.

"Because it just ain't. Take this guy in the poem. All that money and clothes and everything didn't do him no good. He was the most miserable one of the bunch, even if he did have plenty of meat to eat. You are what you are, and if you aren't happy with that, then that's your problem."

"And that, my friend, Daniel, sums up that poem about the best I have ever heard. I do have a fancy word for that, but your definition is better than mine."

"What's your word?" Marie asked out of sincere interest, but she was still asking for the whole class.

"The word for the way the townspeople look at Cory is romanticism."

"I thought that meant something like love." Walter was still happy enough with himself that he wanted to be heard.

"Well, that's one meaning. But here, it means something else—seeing the world through rose-colored glasses."

"You mean like wearing sunshades so you can't see the dirt blow on a bad day?"

"You've got it. That is exactly what it is. Thinking something away from you is more fantastic than it really is."

"What about when my grandpa remembers the good old days?"

"So what about that?" Mr. Benalli asked so gently.

"Well, they didn't have a bathtub or a TV or a car or nothing. How could that be the good old days?"

"I think you are beginning to understand it now. So what about this guy Richard Cory?"

"Well, he sure didn't see things in a happy light. But maybe they weren't as bad as he thought they were."

"So what do you think we ought to call his attitude?" The young teacher was pushing, but if the students could make the connection, it had a better chance of holding long enough for them to put it away safely.

Marie answered again. "Well, it really seems to be kinda pessimistic."

"That's a good word for it." Mr. Benalli acted as if she had invented it herself. "So let's review. What's romanticism mean?"

"Things ain't as good as you think they are." The statement smacked of the country idiom, but it was too full of meaning to undergo correction just now.

"So what does pessimism mean?"

"Things are pretty rotten, but maybe they aren't as bad as you think they are."

By now, the teacher was almost leading cheers with his questions, both in voice and body movement. "And what is Edwin Arlington Robinson trying to show us in this poem?"

"What happens when these two attitudes run into each other."

"What happens then?"

"Maybe they're both wrong. Maybe they need to balance out a little bit."

"Maybe so," the teacher reasoned as he backed out of the discussion to survey what had happened. "And what line will you remember from this?"

Twenty-six voices rang in unison, or as close to unison as twenty-six high school juniors could ever get, "And Richard Cory went home and put a bullet through his head."

One lone voice added, "And Richard Cory, one calm summer night, went home and put a bullet through his head" as if to remind them all that even the weather report was subject to colored glasses.

Sensing a cooperative spirit and a teachable time, Mr. Benalli moved into phase II. "I'll tell you what let's do. I would like for you to write me something, anything, about a time when you had a romantic attitude. You were really expecting something to be great, and it turned out less than wonderful when you met the real situation."

In unison, twenty-six sheets of paper came to the desk tops, and only questions of form interrupted the silence of the next thirty minutes.

Walter asked, "Hey, could this be a poem?"

"Sure."

"Could I make it iambic?"

"I would really like that. Do you know how to count the syllables?"

"I think so."

Danny asked, "How do you spell limousine?"

And when the bell rang, Walter summed up the class for the whole group with a short outburst of protest. "Oh, no. Not so soon. I'm not through yet. Can we take these home and work on them?"

This wasn't a freak day for Vince, one sticking out from all the others which flow together to make a profession. It was a good day, all right, and there were some bad days. But there were other good days too, lots of them. More good ones than bad ones.

And this thought carried Vince through the community breakfast trial and to school that bright, promising November morning of 1980.

9

In Hope of a Fearless Hero
1 9 8 0

"You've got a visitor." With a secretary like Miss Helen McClurg, Vince really didn't need to eat chili late at night to give himself bad dreams. She could manage that assignment by herself. When the work pool was as slim as it was in Wheatheart, Vince knew it was too much to ask for both competency and tact, but he wondered why he couldn't have one or the other. Of course, Casteel found the lady both, and once again Vince was the victim.

Having a visitor who brought that tone to Miss McClurg's voice was never really good news, and it was particularly bad at this time of day. Vince and the school had just slipped into the early morning lull. Since 7:30, he had checked buses, counted students, found yesterday's lost items, checked Craig Brady's eye, policed the hall, located a substitute teacher, arranged for the pep assembly for Friday morning, thanked Rose for handling a discipline problem, wiped a four-letter word off the mirror in the girl's bathroom, checked for the faint smell of smoke in the locker room, listened to the Spanish teacher lament American arrogance and ignorance of foreign language while watching her address failing slips to the parents of half her students. He had collected permission slips for an

FFA field trip to a hog-killing plant, listened to excuses, written admits, and maintained harmony in the hall. In the words of the village conscience, he was "keeping the lid on things up there."

Now that everyone was in a classroom with a teacher and information was pouring forth, a lull swept through the empty halls and invited Vince into his office for a few moments of idle reflection before the next bell rang and madness hit again. Daily, he welcomed the lull. Miss McClurg knew that, and she always seemed so pleased when he had an interruption.

"Who is it?" He sensed his tone was less than cordial, and he wished he had it back so the two of them could start off again. The sun was too bright and the wind too still to go through a day with undercurrents.

"That graduate student, Miss whatever her name is. This is her last day and she wanted to check with you before she left us."

"Has it been two weeks already?" This time Vince made it sound cordial, as if to say, "Let's be friends just this once."

She answered merrily, "Time flies when you get older, Mr. Benalli," and he felt like hitting her. Instead, he busied himself remembering the graduate student and her purpose here.

He had met with her when she first came two weeks earlier, but only briefly. It was on the Friday afternoon of the Mangum game and Vince was up to his chest in football details. She was a graduate student at Oklahoma State working on some project measuring student success against teaching styles. She had chosen Wheatheart as the small, rural school doing a good job academically. She wanted to spend two days apiece with five different teachers. Vince helped her pick out the teachers, then forgot about her, seeing her around only occasionally in the lunchroom and rarely in the lounge. But he had checked her vita and remembered snatches: Thirty-one years old. English major in college. Graduate student in Educational Instruction. High school English teacher for five years. Graduate assistant. Divorced.

He walked into his office, greeted the graduate student, pulled out the chair next to her, and sat down facing her just as the management theory books said to do. They both seemed more comfortable with each other than either had expected and the conversation flowed freely. She had a pleasant face with blue, almost innocent eyes. At thirty-one, her figure was nicely between cheerleader cute and forty-six, with enough slimness to make the clothes fit and enough roundness to show some maturity. Even as she sat quietly in the chair facing Vince, her body moved in the little places. She wrinkled her eyebrows, twitched her nose, wet her lips with her tongue, gestured with her slender fingers, and constantly crossed her legs. Her off-blond hair was ruffled just enough to indicate that she placed more priority on a good time than on discretion.

"How did your project go?" It was a trite way to get into the conversation, but Vince couldn't think of anything more stimulating, and besides, he really wanted to know.

"Quite well, thank you. You and your teachers have been so cooperative. I am really pretty impressed with this school. In the words of all those education professors, you run a tight ship."

"Well, we do the best we can." Modesty was not really in Vince's repertoire. In Wheatheart there was little call for it.

"Your teachers really think highly of you."

"Well, thank you. That is nice of you to say."

"At this stage, I am just reporting. They tell me you were an English teacher."

"For thirteen years!"

"And a good one."

"I don't know. Sometimes I'm not sure what that means anymore," and he tried hard not to think of forty-six.

"They tell me you really did a great job of teaching composition here."

"Well, it *was* kind of a specialty."

"I'm interested," and her face showed it, and she crossed her legs and pulled her skirt to a point where it broke just above the knee. "I' an old English teacher, you know."

"Well, I knew you were an English teacher, but I wouldn't call you old." Vince hadn't said anything like that to a woman in years, and he wondered if he was flirting or just being kind.

"Seriously," she went on, "that is the one thing I could never do well—teach kids to write. If I could have taught composition, I would still be in high school instead of chasing a doctor's degree. Tell me, what is your secret?" She formed her hand into a fist representing a microphone and held it close to Vince's mouth. It was bathed in a faint scent of perfume which added even more pleasantness to the conversation.

Despite the stimulation of his sense of smell, Vince managed a professional answer. "Well, I figured out early that a kid needed two things to write a good paper."

"What's that?" she asked, and Vince couldn't tell whether the question showed more interest in the answer or the speaker. He chose the first.

"Confidence and a sense of organization."

"Okay, but how do we teach those things?" Now, she was definitely interested, maybe not as interested as she seemed to be, but interested enough to warrant an answer.

"Well, let's start with organization. I teach students to use a formula. I suppose any formula will do, but I use the Baptist sermon formula." They both laughed, and he was afraid to admit to her that he had ever heard a Baptist sermon, much less grown up on an average of two a week for the last forty years, or that the stuff of those Baptist sermons was so ingrained in him that he couldn't tell where they left off and all other influences of his life began.

Nevertheless, he showed her the three points and a poem, and she wrote it all down like it was something valuable that she should know.

"So what about the confidence?" she asked, studentlike.

Vince hid behind the feeling of an artist dealing with a nonartist and tried to answer as clearly as he could. "Well, there you just have to understand high school kids, and these high school kids particularly. You have to have a sense of what is important to them and what they are afraid of. We talk a lot about individual differences as if they were some product of creation. But I suspect that most of the time those individual differences depend on how kids feel about themselves. I have seen it in their writing and I have even seen it as they play in sports.'' He was beginning to sound really pompous with all his knowledge, but she listened intently, as if she were hearing something completely new and revolutionary. ''You just give them an audience to write for, and then you let them write.''

''Well, from what I hear, you really do understand kids. That seems to be your strong suit.''

''Maybe I've got a fourteen-year-old mind myself,'' he said, hoping to minimize the compliment.

She tried to help him through his embarrassment. ''Remember, I have scientific evidence.'' She still was in her compliment pose, but this was a direct reference to her position as an educational researcher. ''I heard how you took care of that fight yesterday.''

Vince hadn't thought about the fight for at least thirty minutes and her comment shocked him back into momentary reality, but he successfully rejected it, at least for a few minutes more. ''Well, it wasn't really much,'' he replied in an offhanded, aw-shucks spirit.

''You don't think they would have hurt each other?'' Somehow, she was trying to make Vince the referee into a fearless hero. He wanted to help her, to encourage her, but he knew it wasn't honest.

''Oh, no. What's so funny is that by the time they got down to my office, they were already the best of friends again.'' He didn't know how much she had heard about the fight and the outcome, so he just decided to assume that he was in complete charge from start to finish. And he would have been too, except for Casteel. . . .

''Good friends again? They healed their differences fast.''

''Well, that is kind of the nature of our kids here. These are good people. The kids are taught their values pretty early. There are several value schools in a community like this—the church, the wheat fields. The kids have a lot of responsibility early. People trust them with real things and real jobs. They are assets to the families and to the general economy, and they know that. Their community-based values don't let them go too far astray, usually.''

''So they keep themselves in check?''

"Pretty much. They may drink a little beer and make some noise, but basically, they know the difference between right and wrong, and their value system won't let them go too far."

"I've seen that in the classes. They seem to know when to ease up and let the teacher take control."

"That's what I mean. Despite their childishness at times, they are still rooted in good soil. When we talk about following our impulses, we get some idea of a free-wheeling 'Do it if it feels good' mentality. However, if you've got those roots right, there is also an impulse that says 'No' and demands to be followed as much as the other one. What we are trying to do here is to instill them with that 'No' impulse so they won't get so far as to lose sight of where they need to come back to."

"That's profound. I don't think I have ever heard it expressed like that."

Vince could have gone on like this for hours, but he decided that it was time for him to change course. He did not want to risk losing the spirit which united them by coming across as self-centered. "Well, tell me about your research. What did you find?"

"Well, of course, I don't know yet. I have observed the teachers and written reams of notes. And I finally persuaded your secretary in there . . . "

Vince interrupted her with a chuckle which meant, "I know just what you mean."

"As I was saying, I persuaded her to let me check the Iowa scores. Now, I just have to put all that together, and see if I can draw any conclusions."

"Oh, how soon will that be?" Vince sounded professionally interested in the results.

But her attitude was still closer to that "you big, strong man" game she had played so well throughout the conversation. "Well, I am staying at my friend's apartment down in Alva while she is out of town. If I had some help, I might get at it even tonight."

"What kind of help?" Vince wasn't professional anymore, either.

"Oh, somebody to drink my coffee and maybe hold my hand. I

try to be a good hostess even when I am working." And with that, she pressed a small note in his hand and walked out, stopping only once to glance back over her shoulder with one eye looking peek-a-boo through a small tuft of hair, and a little smile wrestling with the corners of her mouth.

As she disappeared around the corner of the outer office, Vince checked the note in his hand, half afraid of what he would find. It was there, all right—the address of an apartment up by the college in Alva.

10

When Time Stands Still
1980

A quick call to Beth Ann at the bank cleared the evening for Vince. She understood. He had a school matter to take care of down in Alva. This wasn't unusual. He frequently had to go down to the teacher's college there to meet with officials. Besides, she had her hands full. Someone had called an emergency meeting of the bank's board of directors which might take most of the night. She and Vince could just go their separate ways tonight. There was no question of integrity or purpose or even fidelity. They had been married too long to worry about such things, and their careers offered enough anxiety that they didn't have room for any more from each other.

Vince didn't know how to make plans for the evening because he didn't know what to expect. But he did know that he hadn't felt this way in years, at least not since he had become principal. He stood around in the halls and chatted with students between classes. He even chatted past the bell a couple of times causing some of the students to be late, but he did drop into the rooms to explain to the teachers. It seemed to make the kids feel important to have the principal run interference for them.

His whole body felt young, like it had felt years ago when as a young coach he played basketball against his own team and showed those young admirers the moves which had made him college all-conference. He caught himself looking at his own reflection in the windows of the classroom doors; he saw or imagined a straight line from his chest to his belt. "Not bad for a principal," he thought.

He went out behind the bus barn to the hedgerow and picked the last remaining rose of the season, shook off the dust from yesterday's blow, and presented it to Miss Helen McClurg without a single word of explanation.

He stopped by shop class and talked football with Coach Rose. Although the coach was as friendly and as aloof as always, Vince felt that he had a better grip on Friday's championship game, if and when it came up during breakfast conversation tomorrow morning.

Vince had an urge to linger a bit and talk about personal and philosophical things, but neither he nor Coach Rose had the time, and his feelings weren't the right stuff for that kind of discussion between two grown men, even best friends.

He went over to the superintendent's office to talk with Mr. Casteel. Once there, he leaned back in a chair, rested his feet on top of the official school board table, and gave his opinion of the good and bad teachers and what math books they needed to order for next year.

He was having so much fun being principal that the day went quickly, but at times not quickly enough. Anticipation is a strong motivator and a demanding master, and it played both roles to stardom for Vince that day.

The sun set clear, turning the whole western sky into a huge mass of orange and azure. Brilliant colors covered the horizon from the Red River to the Kansas border and lingered for a long time after the sun had disappeared. That was a good sign. The night promised to be even more beautiful than the day, as if that were possible.

Vince changed into his most casual slacks and put on his favorite fall sport shirt. There was no need to wear a tie or be too formal when he was just going to sit around and drink coffee and go over some dull statistics. He started his trip to Alva earlier than he should have.

In the midst of that quiet which unfolds when the day's light and activity turn gradually into the peace of night, Vince drove along the familiar highway, noticing things he had not noticed for years—some late fall wild flowers which had survived the first frosts; cows grazing on the hills, moving their mouths from left to right as a symbol of good health and natural order; and the old one-room, rock schoolhouse standing stately on a small hill, looking as if it were still in charge of the community, even though it had been vacant for more than thirty years.

Then Vince remembered Wagner's Pond. He hadn't thought of Wagner's Pond in years. In the old days when he was still teaching and coaching, he used to spend a lot of time out there. For public reasons, he went for the duck hunting. At least that is what he had told them at the Dew Drop Inn and around town; but he had really gone for the introspection. There was something about the water and the stillness which always provided him the climate to sort his thoughts in. Wagner's Pond had been valuable to him once, and he couldn't remember why he didn't visit it anymore. He still had the need.

Since he was early anyway and didn't want to come across as aggressive, and since he was noticing things out of his past this particular evening, he decided to drop by Wagner's Pond just to see if it was as he had remembered. It was a spur-of-the-moment decision, something he wanted to do, almost an impulse. He pulled his car off the highway, drove over the dirt and rock road for more than a mile, pulled through the pasture, and came upon Wagner's Pond, already glistening in the early moonlight.

He got out of his car and walked enough steps away until he could forget that it was there. Then he sat gently on the ground so as not to soil his trousers with the red dirt along the bank and leaned back against a small boulder which once might have been a dinosaur's hip, for all he knew. Some of the scientists down at the college had made studies of such things, but Vince never paid much attention. He wasn't afraid that such information would challenge his Sunday School teaching. He just didn't have a need to know.

Quietly, he lay and watched the stars come out as darkness seized control of what day was left. And how the stars come out on clear November nights in the middle of the space called Oklahoma prairie! They stretch across the sky bounded only by the four walls of the almost endless horizon. Bright and close. Dim and distant. Familiar stars, some set in patterns Vince had loved since his earliest memories, the Big Dipper, the Little Dipper, the Pleiades—called the Seven Dancing Sisters in Indian country. Unfamiliar stars. Twinklers and glisteners, and the Milky Way so full of stars that they all surrender their individuality and run together to form an inseparable community. "There might be prettier places in the daylight," Vince thought, "the Colorado Rockies or the California coast. But for sheer natural beauty, nothing equals an Oklahoma November night."

Vince shared his time between looking at the stars and throwing pebbles into the pond. He timed and placed his throws so that the ripples interacted with each other. When the smaller ripples from a smaller stone endured and overtook and replaced the bigger ripples from a bigger rock, Vince found himself cheering for the underdog.

It was a good time, a good place to be, a place of endless boyhood where a man could forget what it was he needed to do to forget that he was forty-six and middle-aged and a high school principal committed to keeping the lid on.

After all, forty-six isn't all that bad when time stands still. Maybe it takes a certain degree of maturity to appreciate still times. He was definitely old enough to lie comfortably between the stars and the water, and he almost dreaded the cause which would hurry him on to the night's business.

There wasn't anything right about this whole evening. He knew that. Even though he was going just for the excitement of being flirted with, and had set his limits there, there was no way he could justify it. And it wasn't just the commitment he had made to Beth Ann—it was bigger than that. It was bigger than both people and commitments. It was the reason why you make commitments in the first place, so that life can be ordered and clear. It isn't so much a matter of knowing what you stand for. Rather, it is knowing why you have to stand for something at all. It is the purpose behind the reason. And that purpose was almost too big for Vince to get his mind around. Oh, the preachers tried to help him at times, and once in a great while, he thought he caught a glimpse. The poets helped too, but they weren't always sure themselves. But here, as close to Eden as he had ever been, Vince thought maybe he was beginning to understand what God made man for.

It was like those stars. There was more there than beauty. That's where the poets went wrong, people like Wordsworth and Shelley and Whitman. For them, those stars were art objects, aesthetic material, to be appreciated, enjoyed. Sure, anybody could have seen the beauty on a night like this. But there was something behind that beauty. The stars demanded attention. They conveyed an order and a purpose beyond people or commitments or meaning itself. It was like the North Star, glittering majestically just above Vince's head. That was a beautiful star all right, but it was more than that. It showed men where to go; it pointed the way; and Vince thought of the thousands of people, hearty people who had taken their ships to sea with nothing except their faith in the location of that star—Columbus, Ericson, the navigators of the *Mayflower*. Still after all these years, there it was just above him, almost close enough to touch if he stood on tiptoe as tall as he could.

And those stars pointed the way to God. . . . Vince rolled the word *God* through his mouth several times. But even then, after all the repeating, it was still full of power and majesty. And he lay for several minutes staring both at the water and sky and thinking of that Word and that Idea. He hadn't ever been in a cathedral, but he couldn't imagine a more meaningful house of worship.

He remembered the beauty of Genesis. In the beginning God made the heavens and the earth. This was more than mere myth like the *Iliad*. This was a statement of fact, obviously clear tonight. But it was more than that. It was a promise. God had created it, had put it in motion, and now He was principal of the motion.

Vince knew those things, like he knew that Mark Twain had written *Huckleberry Finn* or that van Gogh had cut off his own ear. But on rare moments, like tonight, he knew those things clearly enough to feel the meaning as well.

But there was still more than what he knew, even tonight. It was like a sentence he was trying to diagram when one of the words wouldn't parse. There was something else to understand in this whole business of being principal and being spiritual and being forty-six all at the same time. And that night in the moonlight by the edge of Wagner's Pond, he prayed for that understanding.

This time he did not search his pockets for a scrap of paper or a chance pen. Despite the moon, the night was too dark and the moment too special for him to write something to add to the dresser drawer!

> O Creator of heaven and earth:
> In the midst of the mighty,
> You are the mightiest because You made it all.
> In the midst of majesty, You are the most majestic
> because You poured it full of majesty.
> In the midst of wonder, You are wonderful
> because You created wonder.
>
> But now, Lord, it has come undone, that which You made,
> Not the stars, nor the sky, nor the land, nor the water,
> But me.
>
> In the middle of all this order, I fly apart.
> Like an overripe wheathead shattered by a hailstone,
> I fly in all directions, scattering myself about,
> and nothing takes root or grows.
>
> O Lord, somewhere in that fertile field of humanity,
> may I plant a seed—just a small seed of significance,

so that I may know that my being here
makes a difference!

As Vince spoke aloud but softly, the moonlight reflected off the
water and a gentle wind blew his words away.

Finally, he hoarded in enough moonlight to read his watch to see
if he had killed enough time, and discovered that it was 2 A.M. So he
got back in his car and drove slowly home, trying to get a grasp on
the meaning of this evening and the day which had gone before.

He recalled something he had memorized once: "I have seen all
the works which have been done under the sun, and behold, all is
vanity and striving after the wind." But since he couldn't remember
the source, he put it out of his mind and tried to notice more of the
night.

11

Testing the Taproot
1980

Beth Ann's board meeting had not been a night under the stars. That was for sure. She had been dreading it all day, ever since Oscar Pritchett, Jr. had called to tell her that he thought they ought to have a meeting.

"Just want to air things out and get on top of the situation." He had tried to say that casually, as if not to cause alarm or make accusations, but Beth Ann knew him and the rest of the five-man board well enough to know that they had some purpose.

As chairman, elected forever or until death, Oscar was a fair representative of the other men on the board. His father, an original homesteader and one of the most successful businessmen in the history of Wheatheart, had not only made a fortune during certain opportune times. He had also accumulated some political cronies along the way, important people, congressmen, and even a governor. In the late thirties, as the farmers were trying to dig out from under the silt left from the dust bowl days, and as the Roosevelt economy brought a sense of optimism to the prairie, Oscar Sr. led the petition for the second bank charter in Wheatheart, and backed his own movement by purchasing about forty percent of the original stock. One Pritchett or another had been the leading stockholder and chairman of the board ever since.

Oscar Jr. had inherited both wealth and business sense. Although he was officially retired, having moved in off the farm several years ago, he made being bank chairman into an almost full-time job, except of course during a couple of months in the winter when he was down on Padre Island.

So Beth Ann wasn't really surprised by his call. She had more or less expected it, or she would have, had she had time to think about it. She had been too busy with bank business to worry about the board of directors. Not only were the examiners coming over the weekend, but loan applications flooded in every day. It was the same story. Small-time operators saw an opportunity to become big-time operators in the oil fields. All they needed was the capital to get started. It was a safe loan, secured by equipment and enough work to make everybody rich and happy. Beth Ann poured over each application thoroughly and deliberately. One by one, she rejected them. The pattern continued with such momentum that she had almost begun to doubt herself. She knew what would happen. When she rejected their applications, these people, her customers, would go somewhere else to get the money. She knew the determination of a dream growing out of a seed of hope. She had seen that too often. There was money available, and as determined as these people were, they would get it. But at least, Beth Ann reassured herself, she wouldn't be responsible for the heartache and embarrassment, for the loss of confidence and pride, if any of the dreams did fall through.

She was confident that she was right, but she couldn't prove it; and now she had an emergency meeting with the board of directors. Since she really didn't know what to expect, or didn't want to admit to herself that she did, she took the time that afternoon to put together some figures, a five-year history of the small but steady progress, the stability, the good report from state examiners and lending banks, and some comments from grateful customers whom the bank had helped achieve their dreams. She didn't know what direction the meeting would take, but she wanted to be ready for anything.

Oscar and the other board members came equipped with a friendliness and cheerfulness which seemed artificial. So when Oscar asked for any old business before they took up the new, she grabbed the opportunity to suggest some remodeling and new furniture she had been wanting. At a normal meeting, it would have taken two hours of persuasion and discussion for these thoughtful gentlemen to come to any kind of agreement on an issue such as redecoration. But not tonight. Their false agreeableness carried right into the vote and within five minutes, Beth Ann had won approval to redecorate. At least, she had accomplished something, regardless of how the rest of the evening went. Inside she chuckled at her achievement, her sense of timing; and that feeling gave her the composure to go into new business.

Oscar opened with a brief introduction which seemed longer than it was. "Well, we, I mean I," he changed the pronoun in the middle of the sentence. But he didn't have to, not for Beth Ann's sake. She knew that the five men had already had their meeting somewhere else, the Dew Drop Inn or the John Deere store, or wherever men meet to talk business before an official business meeting. She knew he meant "we" and she resented them all for it. This meeting had already closed, and they hadn't even heard her side.

Oscar went on. "I've been thinking about Wheatheart here. Just thinking that, by golly, it looks like this little town is about to take off. I see a lot of signs around. New houses. Fences around those farms the best I've ever seen in this country." His comrades nodded agreement, as if it were a valuable insight, something they'd observed but never thought of. Oscar continued. "Yep. I really believe we are going to progress and we, I mean I, just want to make sure that we here at the bank are ready to get in the battle." He laughed at himself when he said it, probably because he thought it sounded like something either Coach Rose or General Patton would have said, and that gave it credibility.

"What do you think we are going to need?" Although she knew

where this was leading, Beth Ann moved cautiously.

"Well, resources, of course." The comrades nodded agreement again and repeated the word as if it were rare wisdom.

This gave Beth Ann the opportunity she was waiting for. She brought out the figures, hard cold facts, and she took the board through the fact sheets deliberately, showing the progress the bank had made under her leadership. Although they had seen those figures before, and some probably had them almost memorized, they were still visibly impressed to see them again all laid out in concrete columns and rows.

She ended her presentation with a strong proclamation. "We have the resources."

After the round of standard congratulations and appreciations, Oscar went on. "Well, we need to make sure we've got the right attitude to go with our resources."

Beth Ann could have directed her comments to any one of the five, but she chose to stare right at Oscar. He had the most confidence. She didn't much want to do battle with an inferior opponent. She wanted to take on the toughest. "What's the right attitude?"

He stammered as he searched for an answer. He had the right answer on the tip of his tongue, but he didn't want to use it, not now, not by himself. He wanted Beth Ann to say it for him, but when she refused he had to beat around, looking for something kinder than the right answer. "Well, we've got to stand behind progress when it comes our way."

"And what is progress?" Beth Ann gave no hint of letting him out of the pressure. In fact, she was enjoying it.

"Well, you know. New stores and buying farms and, and, and . . ."

"And oil field equipment?" Although she wasn't finished with her game, she gave in to save time.

"Well, yes," and they all nodded agreement as if to say that they had finally arrived at the purpose of the meeting. "We understand there have been some applications."

She agreed. "A lot of applications."

"And the board didn't get to see any of them?" Oscar asked like he was either surprised or disappointed.

Beth Ann clarified her position. "You've asked me before to screen loan applications for you. And you have always trusted my judgment. That is what I am doing now, screening applications. So far, I have rejected everything. They have all been bad business. Unstable."

"Now, Beth Ann, we're not blaming you." Oscar's comment was like her father punishing her for spilling her milk at dinner. "But there's big money in oil. These guys are going to bring a lot of business to town. There's a lot of work around a well. Lot of chances for big dollars."

Beth Ann answered as one banker to another. "I know there is big money in oil. But there is stable money in farming."

Another board member, a farmer, welcomed the opportunity to get Oscar off the hook and to say something about the need for the hearty spirit required in his profession. "I don't know about that. Farming is the biggest gamble I know of. Every year you stick those seeds in the ground out there and just hope that by the grace of God they grow and that the dry weather and bugs don't get 'em before you get 'em back. Seems pretty risky to me."

"Yes," Beth Ann was ready for that from at least one person in the group. "But there is something stable about just having that dirt to put those seeds in, and having that dirt makes the people stable, too."

Another board member offered the thought that all the others were thinking and that probably had brought them together. "Maybe, Beth Ann, you just need to know more about this oil business."

"Are you suggesting that I don't know how to do my job?" She was calm, but convincing.

Oscar interrupted as if he were trying to step between them. "Oh, no. You are very competent. You are good for the town. But we do have to have the right attitude. We want to make money when it's thrown right on our doorstep."

"I assure you, I won't turn down any good loans while we still have resources to make them." She had convictions, strong feelings. She just didn't have the facts, not to support the future. She only had facts to prove that she had been right in the past.

"Perhaps," another member suggested, probably for the whole group since his comment sounded rehearsed, "if you don't understand the oil business enough to make decisions about how to get into some of that money, you ought to consider stepping aside."

"What are you asking?" She directed the question to everyone. Oscar stepped between them again. "Oh, we're not suggesting anything. We are just wondering if we are missing the boat here."

Beth Ann regained her composure and made her final announcement. "You have elected me president of this bank. I have an obligation to you, but I have a bigger obligation to the people who have put their trust in me and this bank. And I am going to stay right here and fight for those people with what I know, with what I feel, for as long as I can. When you decide that that isn't good enough, you can fire me; but until then I will be right here screening loans and running the business the best I know how. Don't ask me to step down, because I am not going to, not by my own choice." Slowly and deliberately, she looked around the room, making extended eye contact with each man, each director there, and especially with Oscar Pritchett, Jr. She wasn't really trying to be dramatic. She just wanted to make sure there wasn't any doubt about her position. She wanted each to know that she was firm. Even without the facts, she was firm, and she wasn't afraid to fight the pressures which tried to blow her away from her roots bedded deep in Wheatheart soil.

Though the board didn't agree with her, they understood her. Some feeble attempts to reestablish the pre-meeting false friendliness and cheerfulness embarrassed them all, so each dismissed himself and disappeared into the night. Beth Ann knew they would probably reconvene elsewhere and analyze the meeting, and in some ways she resented it. But she couldn't worry about it too long. It was already past midnight, and she had to get home to see how Vince's night had gone.

She was happy to discover that she had beat him home. "He probably stayed over at Alva to talk business or old times," she thought, "and he needs that kind of conversation." She could sense that he was feeling down lately, but she didn't know why; and even worse, she didn't know what to do about it. At times like these, when she tried to think in terms of husband and wife, she often remembered a trip to an irrigation project up in the Panhandle. The farmer had dug several ditches instead of one big one. At regular intervals, he would open the gates of a specific ditch, and refreshing, nourishing water would run down and feed the plants in that row. Then he would close those gates, open some others, and water the plants in another direction. It was all an exact science with him. He could control the water to any given plant. He knew just what it needed and when it needed it. She thought that their marriage was like that field. She and Vince were watering a whole crop of different kinds of plants, all growing at the same time. Some, in order to grow healthy, needed water from the ditch she flowed down; but other plants, other parts of Vince's life, needed water from ditches she couldn't reach or maybe didn't even know were dug yet.

She was thinking about this, these plants she couldn't water, when Vince came home; they exchanged brief greetings, and went off to bed. Once there, he hugged her emphatically and continued to hold her throughout most of the night.

12

Keeping a Lid on Things
1980

It didn't matter who was waiting in the principal's office this day. Vince needed his early morning lull, and he wasn't going to be interrupted. So far, it had been a horrible day and the first period had just begun. Besides, he was feeling his age, and he wanted either to forget or to feel sorry for himself. Right now, he needed his office.

First, Beth Ann gave him a brief report of her board meeting of the night before, and he reacted with a flush of anger he didn't really understand. He didn't really know enough about the banking business to support her position, but she was his wife and he instinctively defended her.

The breakfast conversation at the Dew Drop Inn had been demoralizing. It always was, but today had been worse than usual. When he got to school, he learned that a teacher was sick, and he couldn't find a substitute. A bus had a flat tire and was late. It was just Wednesday and already spontaneous pep assemblies kept breaking out in the halls. When he yelled at the kids for it, they looked at him like he was Scrooge's grandfather. Some boy stopped up a toilet stool with notebook paper and then flushed water all over the bathroom floor. And Miss Helen McClurg reminded him that he hadn't sent the eligibility list for the state championship game only three days away.

Forget the lull. Once he got into his office he might just lock the door and stay all day. That ought to show them—the students, the bank directors, the whole town. But just about the time he had settled in for a moment to reflect on his pond experience, there were two knocks on the door and Mr. Casteel came barging in like the ogre in a nightmare.

"We need to talk." Casteel rarely had time for such amenities as greetings or expressions of care.

"Okay." That wasn't what Vince wanted to say, but he had little choice.

"The board met last night." As often as he could, Casteel led with this piece of information. It gave his own personal dictum community backing.

"I know. I thought about coming, but I had something else to do." Part of that wasn't true. Even if he hadn't had anything to do, he wouldn't have gone to the board meeting. He used to, but not anymore. He had lost his enthusiasm for such things. Some years, the board consisted of Casteel and five yes-men, and that scene was dull. Other years, when board members weren't yes-men, debates were endless, tedious, and malicious, and that was also dull. But Vince still felt that he needed an excuse.

His absence didn't bother Casteel. Board members never listened to the principal anyway. "Well, they just wanted me to remind you of how important this week is."

"Yes, sir. I am well aware of how important this week is." He could play that game.

"Well, these old kids may have to be taken down a notch or two before it's over. They get too big for their britches, sometimes." Without clichés, Casteel's speech would have been uneventful.

"So you want me to keep the lid on things." Vince meant it as a joke, but he knew how it would be taken.

"Exactly. We just don't want anything to happen to upset the routine and ruin this great opportunity we've got here.''

Vince wanted to respond, "Like a fight in the hall," but he didn't have the courage. He didn't see any need to force the undercurrents to the top.

Casteel went on—Vince knew he would. The man couldn't tolerate silence, except from other people. "This sure is important to us. Good for the school. Good for the community. This is just good for education. To win the state. I can't think of anything more important than that. We're talking best in the state of Oklahoma. That's important, all right.''

Vince agreed and more. "Yes. Some of these kids are going to have a busy month. The seniors have to take the ACT tests a week from Saturday.''

Casteel nodded agreement reluctantly, but added his obvious commentary. "First things first. Let's worry about that game Friday night. I'll tell you one thing. You get a lot more coverage in the *Daily Oklahoman* for winning football games than you do for taking ACT tests.''

Vince listened half-heartedly and tried to remember the conversation which had taken place in his office during that same lull the day before; but it seemed further than two decades ago. Could this be the same profession? Could he be the same man? But he didn't have time to dwell on those questions. Casteel was still spewing forth instructions, reminders, and orders.

"You've got the buses all lined up for the pep club? I am sure Rose has all his details worked out. He always does. Have you sent in the eligibility list? When you get into the playoffs, those things have to go in every week, you know. I guess we had better announce that school will be out at 12:03. Some parents will want to pick their kids up from school. Make sure the teachers call roll for that first afternoon class. We want to get credit for a day taught. Watch out for little problems, things like cheering in the hall. We just can't let something like that get started. I've always thought the best way to handle that kind of stuff is just embarrass them in front of their friends. Take the wind out of their sails and let them paddle by the seat of their britches. Like you said awhile ago, just keep the lid on tight. We'll be all right. This sure is an important win for us. We want everything to stay on an even keel. We owe that to our players. This sure is going to be good for our school and good for education," and so on and so on.

Around some people it is easier to daydream than around others. Despite his tendency to be loud, Casteel still droned; and besides, Vince had a lot to spend his attention on this particular morning. Some personal topics invited his complete attention, while others flitted across the horizon of his mind almost as if they were ashamed to come into clear focus.

But something in Casteel's tone pulled Vince out of his own mind and back into the reality of the lecture at hand which was consuming what was left of his fleeting lull time.

Casteel continued with his interpretation of the school board report. "If we win, and we may as well prepare for it, we will have the victory assembly in the gym at 2:30 Sunday afternoon, so you had better get ready for it. Art Garland will M.C. the thing, since he is the mayor this year, and he seems to be taking care of all the details. He plans to get Brother Bob to do a prayer. I think that's appropriate. You won't have to say anything at the program. Just make sure everything is set up."

"Sounds good to me." Vince remembered having said something about that very issue sometime during the week, but he couldn't place the situation immediately and he chose to ignore it.

"Oh, by the way. Art would like to read a little piece at the ceremony, kind of give the thing some class. Something humorous but with a good message. He wondered if you would ask the English teachers if they could think of anything appropriate." Casteel said this as he was walking out, but it was important enough to him to hear the answer, so he came back in and looked at Vince, for what might have been the first time in the whole conversation.

The only quality in Vince's answer was meekness. There was no need to remind Casteel that he was first and always an English teacher himself. "Yes, I'll ask."

Satisfied, Casteel walked out again, but remembering something else, he turned and came back in. But this time, he didn't look at Vince. He made Vince, the principal, look at him, the superintendent.

"By the way, you know that principal's conference?"

Vince helped his memory. "You mean the national conference?"

"Yeah. That's the one."

"What about it?" Vince knew the man had something to say and he was trying to hurry him along.

"Where's it meeting this year?"

"New Orleans, I think. Why?"

"Well, the board thought you ought to go."

"Why?" Vince wanted to make the question longer—"Why this year, of all years, since I have asked for nine years in a row? Why is it suddenly important for me to mingle with other principals and share ideas and problems?" That was what he wanted to ask, but in the name of diplomacy, he repeated the single word. "Why?"

"Well, we just think you have been working awfully hard and doing a good job and need a change in scenery. And we want to reward you for having a good year." And he added as he walked out, "Even if we don't win that ball game Friday night."

The principal's convention in New Orleans the third week in January! Vince leaned back in his chair and tried to grasp the meaning of that, and the potential. He had heard about those conventions before, and he had heard of New Orleans, and he had never really approved of what went on at either one. But he had never been forty-six before either, and this morning he was even more confused than he had been. Last night had been a sobering experience, and meaningful—one which he would remember for a long time. But this morning, he still felt forty-six and alone and promiseless, still undone, and he couldn't go on just looking at that every morning when he turned off the alarm and wondered what he would order from Rosemary and take from Casteel.

New Orleans was a long way from Wheatheart—from all the busybodies and all the gossip and all the talk of moisture and wheat roots and oil fields, and all the commitments and even all the stars. So he began to make plans.

13

Taking Charge of the Dreams
1980

On Friday, school ended at 12:03, just after the teachers had called role in the first afternoon class. At 12:05, Vince walked out of the building, got into his car, and headed toward Oklahoma City. He knew he was seven hours early for the ball game, but he had shopping to do. Actually, he felt a little guilty about leaving early with so much left to do to prepare Wheatheart High School and the rest of the town to move into Oklahoma City's Taft Stadium before seven o'clock. The cheerleader sponsors would have to load and supervise three busloads of girls, Rose would have to get the football team with all its gear in order; and surely someone, acting on the spur of the moment, would create a caravan of thirty, maybe forty, cars and buses so that the whole state would know just what kind of town Wheatheart was—one that took time out to emphasize the important things in life.

If Vince were around, he could help with all this, be a part, be a leader; but even then, he would have to impose his help, and he didn't much want to do that anymore. In earlier years, maybe even last year or the year before, he might have stayed and insisted on his right to help, but not now, not since he had turned forty-six and had realized it. So he drove on merrily, and almost guiltlessly to the City, planning his shopping trip as carefully as a big game hunter stalks his prey.

For Vince, as for most of the people in the state, Oklahoma City held a strange fascination. It was the seat of power, political and functional. Managers of every kind and in every corner of the state would infer a first-name familiarity with the seats of power by calmly announcing, "I don't know the answer to that question. We will have to call the City to find out."

It was the seat of merchandising, not for food and clothes and tractors—not the things you could get in Wheatheart—but for the exotic and unusual; and knowing housewives across the state would infer shopping sophistication when they would show off their new dress or decorator item and comment, "I bought it in the City."

It was the seat of entertainment and a vibrant hub of show business itself, and knowing socialites would infer worldliness when they casually said, "I saw George Jessel once. He was down in the City when they opened the new Myriad."

For Wheatheart, including Vince, the City was always a romantic fling, but still a reality, somewhere between where they lived their lives on a daily basis and what they saw on television. When they watched a sting operation on a cop show, they couldn't tell whether it was real or fantasy until they heard about it happening in the City. Then they knew it was at least possible, but still in the distance. When they heard about the cocaine epidemic, they hung that information around the images of strange and immoral apparitions living in strange and wicked places, until they heard of a cocaine bust in the City. Then they drew flesh and blood on their apparitions.

The City was always invitingly exciting, but particularly so when you were going alone and if your shopping urge grew out of plans for one of those once-in-a-lifetime events, like the senior prom or graduation or a wedding or a week in New Orleans.

Vince, like the rest of Wheatheart, shopped the malls. There might have been superior stores—better merchandise, more competitive prices, friendlier proprietors—but those were for the residents, the people who knew the streets by name and knew how to drive in traffic lights. For the country folk, the malls were shocking enough. "Just think about it! Right here under one roof you find twice as many stores as you've got in all of Wheatheart and Alva put together! Just think about it! Look at that lady over there. She has her kid in a dog harness. Strangest thing I've ever seen. Look at that guy over there smoking a cigarette through that long black filter. I'll bet he's rich. Look at those short skirts. I sure hope they don't come back into style. We've got enough problems as it is. We don't need something like that inviting more. Just think about it. All these people and all these stores and all under one roof. Just think about it!"

Vince thought about it as he stopped at the entrance to check the directory. He was looking for a jewelry store which might either be understanding or busy enough not to care. He rejected his first choice because there were too many customers just standing around close enough to eavesdrop; but the second choice seemed to meet his need.

He was greeted by a lady who had that city look—long fingernails and painted. You didn't see that on the farm women back in Wheatheart. She had lots of makeup that was tactfully placed. Her dyed hair camouflaged its real color. Her smile said either, "I'm your friend," or "You're a sucker for being in here." Vince couldn't tell which. Her appearance defied guessing her age. She might have been as old as Vince, ten years older, or even ten years younger. He couldn't tell, and he wanted to; it would have made this whole event a bit easier.

"Yes, sir. Can I help you?"

"Yes, ma'am." Vince's voice was so soft he could hardly hear it himself, and it sounded strange, as if it belonged to someone else. "I would like to look at some gold necklaces."

"For your wife, sir?" The woman started to move to another counter.

Vince cringed and recalled a Mark Twain observation. This was the curse of being an old English teacher. Regardless of how serious the moment was, you always found yourself remembering some piece of wit from Twain. This time the quotation gave him strength, though. "Man is the only animal that blushes or needs to."

Despite the Twain comment, Vince had to answer the woman's question. "Uh. No, ma'am. No, uh. It's, uh, it's for me."

"Oh." And Vince couldn't tell how she meant that. Even several months later when he thought about this incident, he couldn't tell. Either she was cool and understanding or she was snickering inside, impatient for him to make his purchase and leave so she could run throughout the mall telling everybody she saw about this forty-six-year-old guy coming in and buying a gold necklace for himself.

Whatever her attitude, she was helpful. She showed him a good selection and stood by as he made a decision. He picked a long necklace with a half-moon pendant which hung down his chest and came just to the spot where the gray chest hair turned black. He rejected the shorter chain and the cross, but he wasn't sure why!

Even though he liked what he had bought, and didn't mind spending the $85, when he walked out of the shop, he couldn't help feeling like he was a small boy shoplifting, pleased with his ability to execute the crime, but unhappy with his urge to do it. But he couldn't dwell on this. He was going to New Orleans, and he still had things to buy.

The shirt was next, but this was easy. He knew exactly what he wanted—a light blue silk with glistening flecks—and he knew where to get it, in one of those special shops which sold only shirts. This time the middle-aged clerk was matter-of-fact, efficient, and almost terse about it. If anyone was crazy enough to pay $65 for a shirt, it didn't matter to him what the customer was going to do with it. In fact, the clerk looked like he had been on a few trips to New Orleans himself.

Vince wished buying the pants would be that easy, but he knew it wouldn't. For one thing, he had never seen designer jeans anyplace except in special stores with catchy names designed to trap the teenagers—names which sounded more like a rock band than a clothing store. And those shops were always papered with the signs of youth—posters and slogans suitable for fourteen-year-olds. And they were always staffed by a whole flock of girls who looked younger than his cheerleaders, and he knew those girls didn't have good sense. Not after the problems he had had with them all week.

Besides, this time he would have to try the pants on and he didn't look forward to that possibility, changing his clothes in one of those phone booths with the door sawed off at the bottom, exposing his bare shins.

But he remembered the words from the television jean commercials, and sucked in his stomach as far as it could go and made his safari into a wild and frantic jungle he had never dared enter before. He tried to be inconspicuous; the young, very young, disco-dressed clerk acted as if she preferred it that way. Always standing with his back to the door, he found the brand he was looking for and started rummaging through for the right size. "This should be easy," he thought. "They have got a wide selection." But he couldn't find the 38 pile. He thought he had overlooked it, so he rummaged through the stack again, and again, but this time more thoroughly. Still nothing with a 38-inch waist. The largest they had was 36.

By now, his shuffling had attracted attention, and the clerk ambled over, blowing a bubble with her gum as she came. "Can I help you, sir?"

"No. I am not really finding what I am looking for here." He made it sound as if the styles weren't right. "Are there stores around with a wider selection?" He was twice, maybe three times the age of this girl and he had a right to put her on the defensive for a change. Besides, it wouldn't bother her as much as it did him.

"Pant stores are all up and down the mall, mister." And with that, she walked away, still massaging her gum into position for the perfect bubble.

Vince tried them—every one he could find, and he had the same luck. No 38s. Finally, in desperation, he mustered his courage to ask. It was a humbling experience, but he was desperate. In normal circumstances the child clerks would have been his students, and he would have been the person in charge, managing their attitudes and even their emotions; but here the roles were reversed, and he was uncomfortable. He was beginning to get a sense of what a student must have felt like when he failed to do his homework or had lost his book and had to tell the teacher. So like the guilty boy caught scuffling in the hall, Vince hung his head, studied his shoe tops in the carpet, and asked, "Can I find these in size 38 somewhere?"

The clerk was helpful, if not friendly, and she told him about a "store for stout men" up on the other side of the city. He could look there. That was the only suggestion she could think of.

So as Vince drove across town, judging the red lights and weaving in and out of traffic, he felt almost at home in the City. Here he was. Running over to the other side of town to pick up a pair of britches because this other store had exactly what he wanted. He liked the ring of that, the way it sounded—but then he realized that he could never tell anybody, couldn't brag about it down at the Dew Drop Inn or in the teacher's lounge. This simple act, driving across the City to shop, was enough to set him up above the others, to hold him aloft if only for a moment, and he couldn't use it. Living out forty-six had a lot of complications.

But he found the jeans, just exactly what he wanted and in his size. They fit perfectly, and he didn't even mind trying them on, not in this store. Here the dressing room door came all the way down to the floor so his bare legs didn't show out from underneath; besides, he was about the smallest and youngest person there. The others, customers and clerks alike, were big enough to appreciate a store especially for them.

Winding his way back through the City traffic, Vince drew mental pictures of what he would look like in his new wardrobe, now hidden away for both safety and secrecy in a remote corner of the car trunk. He didn't know how long he had been in this rather pleasant trance when he first heard the siren. Instinctively, he thought about pulling over to let the emergency vehicle pass, glanced in his mirror, and saw the police car following him. One look at the speedometer assured him of his 25 mph, well within the limit, so the law had to be interested in him for some other reason.

"What could it be?" he thought, and his mind flashed back to the clothes in the trunk and his plans for using them. "Oh, no," he thought, "I'm trapped, caught right in the middle of the City," and he had an impulse to run away, to show that cop some real driving. But his saner being took over. "This isn't illegal. The clothes aren't contraband. These cops don't care." And he pulled over to the curb.

The young policeman strode up to the car, looking more like Earl Bresserman than anything else, and stood as if his power had been threatened. "Hey, Buddie, I just clocked you at 25 miles per hour."

If Vince had had time to think about the situation, he wouldn't have had to sound submissive; but he didn't have time to think about it and submissive was the automatic attitude in situations like these. "Yes, sir, that's what my speedometer said."

"Well, I don't know whether you can read or not, but that is a school zone you just went barreling through."

"A school zone?"

"That's what I said. A school zone, and I am going to write you a ticket for that little act. We've got to protect our children from people like you who don't have any respect for law and order."

And Vince was still submissive. The young officer wrote the ticket, got in his car and left. Vince sat where he was for ten, maybe fifteen minutes before he could regain enough muscle discipline to drive. His heart beat against the walls of his chest; he could feel his face flush, and all the muscles of his body shook involuntarily. Vince struggled with himself. "Why, why am I acting this way? What's wrong? A ticket for speeding through a school zone, that kind of thing happens every day, hundreds of times every day. So what am I afraid of? What have I done?"

He kept asking the question over and over again. It was more than a piece of rhetoric. He really wanted an answer. He needed an answer. He had to have an answer. But he didn't even know to whom to direct the question. Himself? God? Wheatheart?

He felt like he was playing both roles in a student-teacher conflict. For some reason he was a naughty boy, but he was also the teacher who called himself to task.

But what was the mischief? Spending money on frivolous things, doing it in secret, or wanting to do it in the first place?

Could God judge him for trying to find that missing part in his life? Was it wrong to want to know, to scrape off the top layer and look underneath to see the root system, hidden and vital?

Maybe he was shaking in his car with a speeding ticket in his hand because he was afraid the root system wasn't there at all anymore, withered up after forty-six years with too much drought.

Or, maybe he had just lost his courage. Maybe he was too much of a coward to expect any more. Maybe he was afraid of the risk. Maybe he had become so comfortable making safe decisions that now those safe decisions had turned on him, and wouldn't allow him the courage to dream. Maybe dreams all die, not because of age, but because of lack of courage. And that didn't have to be! Not for Vince! He could take charge of his dreams.

He would just act like one of his high school students. They don't have any choice in the matter. They have to dream. In spite of how cocky they might be with the present, they have to know that they are in for a change. Things can't go on forever like this. So they dream! And then they risk the future. Otherwise, they would be stunted the rest of their lives.

Vince didn't want to be stunted at forty-six, or be locked in at this level. He couldn't go back, regardless of how good the past was. So he had to go forward. And that meant taking a chance, like buying a new costume to wear to the principal's conference in New Orleans in January. This was what he had achieved so far today, and he should be pleased, not shaking by the side of the road.

With this reasoning, Vince regained his confidence, drove on to Taft Stadium where the rest of Wheatheart had already gathered to watch the Wheatheart Whippets defeat Tuttle for the state football championship. It was a typical Rose victory, designed and executed deliberately. The plays weren't flashy and the players weren't showy, but they all functioned the way they were expected to. Nothing unusual, nothing extraordinary. Deliberate execution of the orthodox. That's the stuff of championships and champions.

But not for Vince. The trip to New Orleans hung like a brilliant light over the entire evening and tinted the whole affair with a warm glow, the kind of excitement that grows out of anticipation rather than out of the moment at hand. Officially and personally, he hugged the cheerleaders, and congratulated every player individually, even the second and third stringers who sat quietly elated in the shadows of the dressing room. Then he shook Rose's hand vigorously, sincerely, and almost affectionately.

That same glow illuminated the victory celebration assembly Sunday afternoon. Although Vince's only responsibility was being around, he participated in the spirit. Art Garland, acting both as mayor and John Deere salesman, dressed the accolades in appropriate clichés, and entertained the crowd with jokes gleaned from recent vintage *Reader's Digests*. After the players and the cheerleaders and the coaches and sponsors and the band members had all been introduced, and Coach Rose had made his speech attesting to his humility and his dependence on a power greater than us all, Art Garland read the poem, "Casey at the Bat" and drew a patriotic analogy to Wheatheart football. This was his own idea. He had rejected the English teacher's suggestion, "If" by Rudyard Kipling, and Vince's anonymous suggestion, a select passage from Wordsworth's "A Few Lines Composed above Tintern Abbey." But Vince didn't mind. Art's choice probably fit better; and even if it didn't, it didn't matter.

14

Something Worth Expecting
1 9 8 1

The weeks between the state championship football game and
Vince's trip to New Orleans moved quickly for both Beth Ann and
Vince, but for different reasons.

Even though Wheatheart was experienced at winning state championships, this accomplishment always made the school year go
smoother and faster. After the students had locked that victory away
for another year, all of them, players and supporters alike, came
home with a vibrant spirit of confidence which spilled over into
school activities, including classes. The patrons didn't complain as
much. They might have gossiped as much, but they didn't complain. In years when the team won, insignificant issues were treated
as if they were insignificant. But in years the team didn't do well,
those insignificant issues could become time-and-emotion-wasting
community perils. Since the students were happier, the town was
happier. Since the town was happier, the teachers were happier. All
except the basketball coach, of course. Mr. Diel, Vince's replace-
ment and a fair coach in his own right, required a lot of tender
attention during those days when he had to put a basketball season
together in a community which was just coming off an extended

football high. But Vince didn't mind spending time with Coach Diel. He was young and eager, and he listened. Besides, Vince could give personal advice, experienced advice; and that is always the easiest kind to give.

But through most days, Vince's mood danced above the good spirit in the school, which he hardly noticed at all. It just seemed normal to him. In some ways, it was a duller year than most, but he entertained himself with thoughts, even dreams, of his trip to New Orleans. He didn't know what the trip had to offer, but he knew something different was going to happen, and that was worth expecting. A child's Christmas had come to middle age. Vince was going to New Orleans.

Beth Ann was just as occupied, except now it was with the present, not the future. Board meetings came regularly, but the tone shifted from indirect to direct. They weren't playing social games anymore—she and those board members and Mr. Oscar Pritchett, Jr. They were all frank. They thought she couldn't handle her job, and she refused to resign. If they felt that strongly about her incompetence—her judgment in this oil field matter—they would have to take definite action. That might have sounded like a dare. Some people around town suggested it did, and told the board so. But she didn't mean it as a dare. She just wanted to put the responsibility on the board of directors. In her own way, without any proof and even with growing evidence to contradict her—the drilling rigs were in place and already punching holes in the ground—she still knew she was right, so right that she refused to quit to accommodate them. The directors, even working collectively, hadn't found the courage to fire her; so she stayed on, supervised the remodeling, ran the bank, opened the records to examiners, and refused loans to purchase oil field equipment.

Both Beth Ann's and Vince's preoccupation with things inside themselves brought them closer together, but only in one sense. They were both alone now, Vince in his fight to escape and Beth Ann in her fight against the obvious, and they needed each other. But neither could tell the other where the anxiety was. They weren't afraid of each other or, at least, neither thought so; but out of respect for each other's privacy, they never touched that point of their lives where each was spending most of his attention. Oh, they knew. Vince knew that the bank directors were angry, and Beth Ann knew that Vince was excited about going to New Orleans. But they didn't know much else. So they confined their communication to diversion.

Now that football season was over, they spent a few evenings with the Roses, hosted the teachers to an open house, went to a couple of Christmas parties, and traveled back to Beth Ann's parents for a short holiday trip. When it was time to return to Wheatheart and their own lives again, Beth Ann's mother made her promise to wear her galoshes when there was snow on the ground. Although Vince didn't understand the full depth of the irony as well as Beth Ann or even Oscar Pritchett could, he still found the promise funny, and that served to draw them closer together, a common laugh about something as poetic as human nature.

Even with their social lives together, there was still that distance of respect, or maybe fear. But the one place where they seemed to find a depth of communion, communion without conversation, was in church. Although they both listened to the same sermons and heard the same points and illustrations, they might have each gotten a different message, so different was their need for the message. But that didn't matter, they were still both working off the common experience, the same church service and sermon; and this structured tight enough boundaries around their thoughts and feelings that they felt closer to each other while listening in silence.

During this time, Brother Bob intermingled the customary Christmas messages into a short series of sermons on the seeds of real faith. Brother Bob was a good country preacher, almost ideal for the Wheatheart Baptist pulpit. He was a bit of a theologian, and something of an historian. But he was mostly a showman, a master storyteller. That was a necessary feature at Wheatheart, where people got most of their information through stories.

For his sermons on seeds that produce real faith, Brother Bob used the classic illustrations—Abraham, who left his home to go to a promised land; Paul, who gave up a career in church politics to become a tentmaking missionary; Noah, who risked his reputation to build a boat which spared the human race; Timothy, who offered himself to the Law so that he could minister to the Jewish people.

For his sermons on the Christmas theme, Brother Bob reminded the congregation that God had come and had planted His seed.

Somehow, Vince's vacuum made Brother Bob seem a better preacher than he really was, and the sermons rang deep through Vince's thoughts and days. He remembered the words of the sermons even after Brother Bob had forgotten them.

The only person who could have known how moved Vince was by the sermons was Beth Ann. During the service, she sat close enough to him to feel him thinking. But she was busy thinking too. And on top of that, Beth Ann and Vince enjoyed those messages together. They talked about the sermons on the way home and over dinner. They even remembered enough to discuss the fine points, bits and pieces of information about biblical examples which one of them had never known before. And yet, through those conversations, some of them quite long even, Beth Ann and Vince sat in their private worlds. Deep within their souls, so deep that it was hidden below knowing, each asked the same question, "What am I reaching out for?"

15

The Meaning of New Orleans
1981

On the third Sunday evening in January, Vince flew into New
Orleans, wearing a navy pin-striped three-piece suit. His silk shirt,
designer jeans, and gold chain were in his suitcase.

By noon the next day, he had discovered that a principal's conference is not unlike a coaching conference. Participants gather for
meetings and meals, and on the coffee shop napkins, they draw
period schedules and curriculum models rather than Xs and Os of
basketball plays. It was all the same, but this time Vince was
different. He would get to the meetings all right, but it was what
came after which would make this time distinctive.

The first night, he rested and charted his immediate future. At
forty-six, he wasn't automatic at such things; it would take some
planning. The hotel itself offered enough fascination to hold Vince
for one evening. Visitors to Oklahoma frequently called it "the
South." Vince had heard that so much he had begun to believe it,
until now. Whatever Oklahoma is, it isn't the South; maybe the
Southwest, or the bottom of the Midwest, or a culture all its own.
But New Orleans is the South. At the hotel, aristocracy oozed out of
the setting and the people, so that you could forget the last 125

years. Antebellum elegance abounded. The hotel structure, both inside and out, might have been designed by the same architect who drew the plans for Tara of *Gone with the Wind*. The furniture contributed to an ambience which spoke of the power and grace of antiquity.

Women moved about in long, flowing evening dresses which carved their figures into the appearance of slenderness; and they spoke with subdued tones, slowed by southern tradition into a distinctive pattern, communicating both elegance and coyness. The men acted as if they appreciated it all.

It was definitely a different world, and Vince threw open all his senses, trying to absorb as much as he could. This was the South. He could tell it with his eyes and his nose and his ears, and with his whole being. This was the night he had been waiting for all winter—well, one of the nights, at least.

The second night, Vince decided to add more memories to his cache. He would spend some time on the infamous Bourbon Street. He could have had company—several of the principals were going and asked him to join them; but this was something he wanted to do alone. He had too many plans to share the night with someone else's needs.

With the care of a knight dressing for a tournament, he put on his new armor—the silk shirt, the jeans, and the gold chain. He opened the second button of his shirt top so the half-moon gold pendant was just visible above the break in the silk. And he walked boldly, expectantly, down the boulevard which led him into the teeming crowd sampling in the novelty shops and bars up and down Bourbon Street. The setting carried him into another world, another time, and he lost track of Vince Benalli and forty-six. New Orleans was even more festive and unreal than the Oklahoma State Fair, and he wanted to make it last forever—the tap dancers on the streets outside the bars performing for the coins tossed by onlookers, the people wandering in and out of the nightclubs, the sightseers riding in the horse-drawn carriages, and those just milling about having a good time. Tonight they were enjoying themselves. Forget about tomorrow or the next day. Plunge in now because this night is all the reality there is. Vince had waited for this attitude for months, and he was ready to make the most of it.

By listening to the quality of the jazz coming out of the open bar doors, he selected the one which seemed to be right, went in, ordered a Coke, took a seat back in a corner which gave him a full view of the proceedings and watched the parade pass by.

Several times during the evening, Vince saw ladies, nice ladies, hard ladies, and tramps come and go in twos and threes. And often he thought about getting up and starting a conversation. But while he was mapping out his opening speech, some burly fellow with an open silk shirt and a gold pendant would come by, whisper in the lady's ear, and they would disappear into the crowd on the street. He felt secure enough to meet some new people, but he just wasn't interested enough to be bold. So after sitting and sipping his Coke for what seemed like half the night, Vince chose to change scenery. Just to make sure he was not out past the hour of human decency, he glanced at his watch and noticed that he had been in the bar a total of sixty-seven minutes. No wonder he wasn't sleepy yet.

He walked out on the street where the light of day had disappeared and the artificiality of Bourbon Street was engulfing the night. At first, he thought the mood was the same he had seen earlier in the evening, but it wasn't. It was more rapid and harsh, more businesslike, and undercoated with an unpleasantness which made even the happiness joyless. Vince walked up and down the street, shocked by what he saw. As the doors to the nightclubs swung open to admit customers hurrying in as if from a sense of duty, Vince caught glimpses of dancing girls in costumes of almost nothing and in positions which would have been indecent even if no one had been looking.

Vince knew he shouldn't be here. It was as simple as that. He didn't even need to explain this to himself.

He still didn't know what was missing in his life, but he knew that Bourbon Street at night wasn't the stuff of real life. He just didn't belong here.

He walked slowly but purposefully back to the security of his hotel. Once there, he stopped in the lobby to take stock of himself and the evening. He was disappointed and would have felt sad, if he had been in Wheatheart where he had the comfort to be sad. Was this what he had prepared for, had looked forward to for all those months? Was this all his forty-six-year-old spirit could put together? How would he now live with himself, now that this opportunity was nothing but memory? The questions bothered him, but he was afraid of their answers, so he searched for diversion, for something to read. The only thing available in the lobby was the huge conference bulletin board. The Meat Market, as it was affectionately called by the regular attenders, was covered with announcements of principals looking for a change in career and lifestyle and of schools looking for principals and assorted administrators. Although his concentration was blurred by more personal pressures, Vince went through the rudiments of reading, pronouncing the words if not digesting the message. Suddenly, one announcement caught his attention. It was brief but friendly:

WANTED—ENGLISH CURRICULUM COORDINATOR

QUALIFICATIONS: EXPERIENCED ADMINISTRATOR
WITH ENGLISH CLASSROOM EXPERIENCE.

CORPUS CHRISTI, TEXAS

CONTACT MR. BENNETT IN ROOM 812

As Vince read, his mood changed from personal to professional. He had heard about such jobs for years; but until now, it had never really occurred to him that a person could be both an administrator in charge of things and still keep one foot in the classroom. This had potential for teachers who moved into administration because they wanted to, as opposed to those who were forced up because they were ineffectual as teachers. It was a possibility for people like himself, whose knowledge in an important teaching field was going to waste. "Why not?" he asked himself. "This is New Orleans. What would it hurt to ask?" So he rushed upstairs to his room, took off his new clothes and stuffed them into a bag deep in his suitcase, showered with an unusually heavy application of soap, and called Room 812.

Vince was impressed that Mr. Bennett was the kind of person who was in during an evening in New Orleans; he was also impressed with the invitation to "Come on down and chat about it."

After seating himself comfortably and rejecting the cup of tea which seemed to be offered as much out of sincerity as necessity, he and Mr. Bennett began the pleasant task of getting acquainted. Both had their turns with credentials. Mr. Bennett told Vince about Corpus Christi—the town and the school—putting heavy emphasis on the weather and the coast with all its advantages. Vince told Mr. Bennett about his degrees and his career, his thirteen years in the classroom and nine years as principal. He didn't mention coaching. With some school agents, coaching would have been assumed as part of the career. In the other districts, coaching would have been irrelevant. In either case, Vince saw no need to mention it.

With the official qualifications satisfied, the two men got down to business. Mr. Bennett, as the personnel director, was good at his job, and Vince was comfortably talkative, perhaps subconsciously relieved from thinking about what might have happened this night.

"How did you feel about yourself as a composition teacher?" Mr. Bennett phrased the most important question in a personal way.

"Actually, I feel that it was my strongest point, particularly in the rural area of Oklahoma where the country kids have fewer opportunities to see good writing."

"Well, I suspect good techniques will work anywhere. I have always discovered that secondary students are about the same wherever you go. And writing is writing. What's your secret?" His tone was encouraging.

"No secret, really. You just have to help the students gain some confidence, and then teach them how to organize their ideas."

"That makes sense to me, but what do I know? I was a science teacher myself. How do you teach students to organize ideas?"

Having been asked, Vince took that opportunity to go into his three-point scheme, but this time he called it an enumerative-thesis outline. After all, this was New Orleans and this man was from Corpus Christi. Somehow the reference to a Baptist sermon didn't seem appropriate, or at least Vince was afraid it might not be.

After Vince's presentation and demonstration and Mr. Bennett's intelligent questions covering the whole writing process, the personnel director from Corpus Christi changed directions. "Tell me, Vince—may I call you Vince?" Vince was hoping he would. That was a good sign. "Tell me, who is your favorite author?"

"Flannery O'Connor," Vince answered without hesitation and then he watched for the flinch; but it didn't come; or if it did, he didn't see it. Although Flannery O'Connor was high on his list of the authors he liked to read when he was in a good enough mood to handle the realities of living and dying, she was not really his clear-cut favorite, even if he had one. But with that answer, Vince had told Mr. Bennett two things. He had told him that he had more than a love for the farm people, simple and complex, common and universal. He felt more than love for them—he identified with them, thought what they thought and felt what they felt. Could a metropolis like Corpus Christi, Texas tolerate a school administrator who looked at his place in the scope of things through country eyes? But his answer also said that Vince wasn't afraid of the Word or the Idea in which Flannery O'Connor rooted her characters.

Knowing full well what he was doing, Vince had blurted it out, and then had looked for Mr. Bennett to flinch, but apparently there was no flinch, because thirty minutes later, after they had talked about Wordsworth and Dickens, and Seneca, the Roman playwright Vince had discovered in recent years, Mr. Bennett asked Vince to come to Corpus Christi for an official interview during the first week in February.

Vince had discovered the meaning of New Orleans—without his costume.

16

Stumbling in the Right Direction
1981

Vince left the warmth of New Orleans and flew back into the worst night of the winter. At 28 degrees, it wasn't the cold—in Oklahoma, it rarely is just the cold alone—but a combination of the cold with a north wind which drove the chill factor down way below miserable. The light mist which fell turned immediately into solid and glazed the prairie with an eerie, glistening, and treacherously beautiful coating, more suitable for appreciating than for driving.

Vince wondered if Beth Ann would even try to come to the airport to pick him up; he half hoped she wouldn't. He didn't look forward to the drive home with all that ice, or even without it, for that matter. But she was there waiting at the gate, and together they made the two-hour trip home in only five hours. Not bad time for a night like this.

Actually, Beth Ann came as much for herself as for Vince. In the last few days, with drilling rigs working around the clock, Wheatheart had turned colder than the weather. The farm customers kept coming in. They had to—this was their bank. But the conversation was always brief and businesslike, terse even. It lacked the warmth that makes for good small-town living.

She was at the airport all right. She wouldn't let a little hazard like an ice storm keep her away from her only friend in town.

Since Vince was jubilant and since he wanted to direct the course of the evening, he carried the conversation early. "How was your week?" Between husband and wife, this was more than a simple greeting. It was a sincere question seeking a thorough answer.

But Beth Ann chose to be affectionately evasive at the beginning. There was no need to ruin an evening with stories he had heard before about things he couldn't comprehend! "You know how it is, Vince. Things never go right when you aren't home."

"What do you mean?" He was half prying for a compliment and half waiting for bad news to fall.

"Well, for one thing, I just can't sleep when you're not home. I never could." She chose to stay in the personal realm.

"Oh," and he breathed more easily with compliment intact. "Me neither. I wonder why that is?"

"Maybe we miss each other." She said that matter-of-factly, as a woman who had been married to the same man for more than twenty-three years.

"But we don't talk all that much when we are home, or at least it seems so at times." Vince wasn't complaining. He too was just stating a fact.

"Maybe we don't have to." She hurried her response. "Maybe we don't have to express a lot of things anymore because we know how we feel."

"Are you implying that we take each other for granted?" He was teasing her.

"No. I don't mean that. I just mean that maybe we are comfortable with each other. We make our world go better. We don't have to talk about it. We just have to be around. There is security in our relationship."

Vince caught the banking allusion; but she didn't, so he dropped the issue and changed the subject. He was in no hurry to get to the meat of this meeting because they still had a long distance to go over hazardous roads. Along the way, as they drove slowly, they passed cars and trucks stranded in the ditches and abandoned for the night or until a heat wave dissolved the peril beneath them. "What do you hear from the school?"

"I think they will all be glad to have you back." She spoke with a Wheatheart "I told you so" tone in her voice which reminded Vince of why it was good to be home with her.

"Why, did they have a lot of trouble?" That question bothered him because he couldn't tell whether he was hoping they had.

"Not anything big. But Casteel just went around the place making a fool out of himself, from what the kids and their parents say." Even with her own problems, she had gathered such information for Vince.

They both laughed and Vince observed, "He and I do make quite a team up there, don't we?"

"Sense and insensibility!" she said softly, and they both laughed again, fresh and easy laughter which warmed the whole of both their worlds.

She stirred the dying embers of spark which the laughter had ignited with an abrupt announcement. "Oh, I've got a surprise for you!"

"Oh, what?"

"Your car is in."

"What car?" He wasn't that forgetful, but he had to delay until his mind came back into the reality of Wheatheart and events of the recent past.

"You know, that Firebird I ordered for you. It came in. I was going to drive it down tonight and surprise you until this ice hit. But you can see it when you get home. It is beautiful—low and sleek like you, baby blue, and the loudest stereo system you have ever heard. Vince, you are going to like it. It may be the sportiest car in Wheatheart." She was prouder of him for having it than of herself for buying it.

Just then a patch of ice on the highway threw their car into a series of uncontrollable spins. Through Vince's skillful maneuvering, he managed to regain control. But the whole incident enabled him to avoid thinking about how he should respond to her gift in the light of the news he had. Perhaps through exhaustion or fright or judgment, he sat silently and riveted his attention to the road in front, searching for those stretches of ice which covered unexpected places.

Beth Ann detected the pregnancy of the silence and couldn't live with it, not this night after they had been separated by a week of time and more than two months of plans and pains. "You act as if you have a surprise for me."

"I do," he admitted eagerly. "It's in my suitcase, but I am not going to tell you and ruin it for you. You just have to wait until we get home."

"Is there something else?" she asked knowingly, and Vince remembered their twenty-three years together.

"Beth Ann, I had a job interview."

"Oh." She was trying to help him tell her, to hide her emotions until the story was out, but she couldn't hide the tone that suggested that she expected the worst.

"Corpus Christi, Texas. Down on the bay." He was trying to be casual but informative.

"A principal?"

"Better than that. Something I have always wanted. An English coordinator." He was excited just thinking about the possibilities.

Now it was Beth Ann's time to study the road intensely as if she could by her own power of concentration increase Vince's skill at the steering wheel. She drew long breaths as if to fill the space in between with more thought, trying to understand what she was feeling and why.

What was her obligation to Vince? This was the happiest he had been in months. She could see that. And she didn't want to steal it. She wanted him to be happy. That was part of her goal, her mission.

But she had an obligation to Wheatheart too, an obligation to fight the forces and the attitudes and the coldness and to cling to what she knew was right when only she believed it was right. Which was the greater debt?

Vince felt the need to continue. He wasn't through telling her, but he wasn't sure how to gain the confidence or organize what he had to say into a proper enumerative thesis. "I really don't know that much about the place. I just talked to the personnel director a while one evening. You know how it is, just sitting around the hotel at night when everyone else is out getting drunk. I just thought it might be something exciting to do. So I went up and talked to him." He paused and with his silence pleaded with her to say something, to ask more questions, to interrupt, or even to scold him; but she stared straight ahead and said nothing. He had to fill the vacancy with something so he went on, stumbling for the right direction. "You know how it is. Just a feeler, really. I just wanted to see what a big city personnel man would think of a country hick principal. He was cordial enough, but nothing is going to come of it. Nothing, I tell you. It was just a lark. Something I wanted to do."

"Vince," she interrupted with a voice so low that it sounded as if pronouncing the words, blowing the air through her lips, caused her pain. "We can't go. We can't leave Wheatheart."

Despite the softness, Vince heard clearly; besides, he had been expecting that decree, wishing it would never come, but knowing it would. But he was too tired and too restless and too excited to accept what he heard, so he blocked it away from his brain and tried to shift the tone into a lighter mood. "You know how it is. He was pleasant to me, but those guys have to be. He invited me down to Corpus early next month. I told him I would come. The trip might be good for me. But nothing is going to come from this. Nothing. They aren't going to offer an important job like that to a country bumpkin."

And she repeated herself, almost. "Vince, I can't go. I can't leave Wheatheart."

With that, they drove the rest of the way home in silence, and the weather stayed icy and frigid for the next two weeks until it was time for Vince to go to Corpus Christi, Texas, to talk earnestly about the new position.

17

The Real Stuff of Pleasure
1981

Corpus Christi was everything Vince wanted it to be. By flying in the evening before his formal interview, he had a chance to look around the city. It was ideal in size, climate, and tone. It was large enough to offer the advantages of a city—live theater, shops, restaurants; and yet, it was small enough not to frighten away a man with an appetite slightly too big for Wheatheart. There was an urban air mixed with the sea breezes, but a country friendliness over it all.

That night Vince walked along the seawall and watched the bay push its waves against the barriers, as if that huge power of water was straining to escape that which held it confined. Without knowing it, he felt like that sea. The water was not quiet here, like the docile pool of Wagner's Pond, content to lie meekly and ripple only when someone made it ripple, and luring the spectator into a mood of tranquility. Here the sea clamored toward the shore, vibrant and alive, carrying in front of it the restlessness of risk.

Vince stood alone on the T-head and tried to coordinate his internal workings with the stars. But he couldn't find any that he could distinguish or recognize. "It's cloudy," he reasoned. "Or maybe the wrong season."

But he was too full of the moment to worry about such things. So he opened his senses and grabbed for as much smell and sound and taste and sight and feel as he could pack deep into his reservoir of retained experiences. "This is the stuff of pleasure," he thought, "the real stuff of pleasure. Even if nothing happens, this night on this pier makes this trip worth the coming and also makes it all right to be forty-six." He wondered how many other people, here and back in Wheatheart, understood the same things he understood and felt what he felt.

But the next day was even more fulfilling than the night had been. The people were as nice as the setting. Since he had had only one other real job interview in his life, and that was twenty-three years ago, Vince didn't know what to expect. But he was delighted. The administrators—from the superintendent to the principals—were cordial and helpful, not terse and aloof. The secretaries, at least those he met, were cheerful and worked at appearing to enjoy their work.

Further details of the position excited him. He would have responsibility and the freedom to carry it out. His administrative duties, if performed well, could make a difference in what happened to students in classes. Most of the time he would be talking with English majors, people accustomed to embellishing their conversations with allusions and quotes from Twain and Wordsworth, and even James Joyce. And maybe, once again, he could find afresh what he had discovered so many years ago and had forgotten—that there is a whole world beyond the Dew Drop Inn breakfast conversation and football teams and fights in the hall.

Through the day, Vince tried to act dispassionate, objective, cool; but he wasn't much good at it. He wanted that job. He wanted to pack his bags and his wife, shake the dust off his feet, and come to this place where he could establish his dreams once again. He wanted that job, and it showed. But even his attitude seemed to encourage the officials. The day began on a high note that grew even louder as the day and the interviewing process continued.

Finally, about two in the afternoon, after the official discussions of such standard matters as duties, salaries, chain of command, Vince's approach to teaching composition and the other components of the English curriculum, the personnel director suggested a rather unusual and challenging idea. They were excited about Vince's theory to encourage students to write and would like to see it in operation. Would he care to run out to one of the high schools where they could borrow a classroom of students so that he could demonstrate his theories in real practice?

Vince welcomed the invitation. He recognized that it was unusual, and he hadn't planned to do such a thing—to perform as a teacher. But he liked the idea and accepted it as a straightforward suggestion without any hidden meaning or any plot to trap a country bumpkin high school principal who proposed to show city English teachers how to teach their areas of expertise, when he himself had been out of the classroom for almost a decade. He welcomed the invitation, until he thought about it.

As he, the personnel director, and the assistant superintendent in charge of instruction drove across town to the school where it was arranged that Vince would demonstrate his skills, he suddenly remembered where he was and who he was. They drove down streets lined with palm trees and past small parks where mesquite stood as sentries to a mysterious place Vince had never seen before. The low houses blended with the sea air and pulled a thoughtful Vince into a Melville world in which he was a stranger except in the faraway reality of reading.

It was then that he realized what he had volunteered to do! He had never taught students except in Wheatheart, and that was different. He knew them. He knew their parents and knew where they lived. He knew what books and magazines they read, what they watched on television, what kinds of skills they had with reading and football and driving a tractor. He knew what made them laugh and cry. And he knew what stars they watched on moonlit nights on the banks of docile ponds.

As Vince thought of his Wheatheart students he tried to imagine the people of Corpus Christi, total strangers living in a strange land;

and he had to catch himself to keep from asking, "They do speak English, don't they?"

By the time they got to the school, a sense of anticipation had already taken over the English department, and Vince didn't have time to think anymore about what he was about to do. He only had time to feel it. Although he hadn't felt this way in nearly ten years, he recognized the symptoms. His palms were clammy, the knot in his stomach was pesky enough to call his attention to it, his voice quivered when he spoke, he caught himself laughing at a remark which wasn't funny or wasn't even meant to be, and he had to find a bathroom. This was the way he had felt before every basketball game his Wheatheart Whippets had ever played in the thirteen years he had been their coach. Euphemistically speaking, he was apprehensive. In plain talk, he was scared to death.

He was trapped by his own volunteering and he didn't know how to get out. This was the test—the Corpus Christi people were going to base their decision on him and his ability to function in their school system on how well he could do in front of a group of students he didn't know anything about. He felt like a newborn baby with his soft spot exposed. But it was all part of a dream anyhow, and tomorrow morning he would wake up in Wheatheart, eat his breakfast at the Dew Drop Inn, listen to familiar conversations, go off to a day of interacting with Casteel and McClurg, and busy himself with keeping the lid on things. He would live through this day and forget as much as he could.

The introductions were simple. This was a writing class of college-bound juniors. This was Mr. Benalli, an expert in the art of writing. They had asked him to show the students a procedure for developing a paper. And with that, the thirty-three students and six teachers who had come in to watch settled back in a less defiant mood than Vince had expected. As he stood and looked out at the sea of strange faces, they weren't all that strange. If he had had time to practice his remembering and imagining, he could have put a name on every face, not a real name but a Wheatheart name. But it would have fit just the same. Oh, there were some small differences in clothes and hairstyles, and maybe not so many callouses on the fingers or so much dirt under the nails, but the similarities pushed the differences into insignificance. Suddenly, Vince was transformed into Mr. Benalli, and the class started.

"Let's imagine," Mr. Benalli suggested with enthusiasm in his style and a hint of tongue-in-cheek seriousness in his tone, "that as your fairy godmother . . ." Subdued laughter rippled around the room showing the teachers there that the students had accepted this new instructor without thinking that he was childish or "hoaky" because of his attempts at humor. Mr. Benalli responded by restating the premise. "Let's suppose that as your fairy godmother, I grant your wish to see the President, and give you five minutes to make one point to him. Now, listen carefully to the rules. You only have five minutes and you can only make one point. Now, what one point do you want to make to the President of the United States?" He paused, caught his breath, and then the answers came, spontaneously and enthusiastically, from all over the room as if the students were saying, "Thanks for asking us this question, for making us think about it, for making us feel that our answers to such a question really matter." As each answer came, Mr. Benalli listened intently and encouragingly, and then carefully wrote it on the board, so that the student would know his comment was worth consideration.

"Nuclear stockpiling is stupid and has got to be stopped."

"We have to support social security and get it out of the mess it is in."

"The federal government has got to control oil drilling practices in the gulf before some big accident ruins this whole coast."

"We shouldn't interfere in the Iran-Iraq mess. Just leave those people alone with their own problems."

"With all the hunger there is in the world, we shouldn't pay farmers not to plant crops."

"I would want to tell the President that schools are better than he apparently thinks they are. We are really learning something."

After he had carefully acknowledged each of the many responses, some thoughtful, some spur-of-the-moment, many reflecting the compelling needs of romantic youth to make the world better, Vince stepped back, as if to assess the importance of the list, and then he asked the next question. "How would you make sure the President heard you? What technique would you use to make the greatest impression so your idea would stand out above all the other ideas he heard that day?" Mr. Benalli bore the silence which followed because he was expecting it. This was a deeper question than the other and needed more time to sink into each student's connecting center where the ideas of the present link up with the ideas of the past to formulate a workable solution. Slowly the responses started flowing in, each person assured of the value of his suggestion.

"I would use statistics and facts. You can't argue with the facts."

"I would tell him a funny joke which would make him laugh, but would make the point."

"I would just keep saying it over and over again. Repetition. That is how we learn."

"I would tell him a parable, something like what Jesus did with the people in the Bible."

Again, Mr. Benalli wrote the responses on the board until each student had had his say. Again he backed away, assessed the list as if he were contemplating a new challenge, and asked, "What would you think if we could come up with a system where we could do all these things? Would that make the point?"

"Yes," they all agreed, if not in unison at least in universal approval; and they waited as if they were about to hear a profound secret and maybe something even a bit magic.

Mr. Benalli assured them, "It's really rather simple. We will begin by stating the point in a clear declarative sentence. That should get the reader's attention. Next, we explain our statement. In this explanation, we are going to use all the guns we have. Statistics, facts, records, reasoning, definitions, logic. Now we are ready for the third step. That is the illustration. Someone tell me how we illustrate the point?"

Short answers peppered the room, indicating that the students were eagerly following each point and rushing to see where this new system would take them.

"Jokes."

"A personal story, something about yourself."

"A parable."

And Mr. Benalli put all their responses below the word, ILLUSTRATE, which he had written on the board.

"Now," he said, "we just have one thing left to do. Restate our initial point. That way we achieve the repetition which is so important, and we leave the President with a clear notion of what our one point was." He looked over this group he had known for at least the last twenty minutes, and felt confident enough to make the assignment.

"Now, we need to try it out. I would like for you to develop that one point you want to make to the President. Write it out according to our scheme here. Then you can see how effective you will be when you do get your chance."

Thirty-three students started to work on an essay worthy of the President or at least of Mr. Benalli.

The responses which came from the spectators, teachers, and administrators were more than courteous, more even than sincere. They were professional—questions about how the system could be adapted to other situations, suggestions for refinement, questions about where the writing could go from here, and several comments about the students' participation in discussion and in subsequent writing. For the first time in a long time, Vince enjoyed being Mr. Benalli in a real teaching role, and not just the one in his memory.

That was the climax. The rest was denouement, and it went without irony. Vince was handed a contract to sign and send back in a week or two.

18

Order in Chaos
1981

Getting a new job and opening his mind to dream again had been easier than Vince had expected. The tough part was yet to come. He had to tell Wheatheart, all of Wheatheart—Beth Ann, the town, Casteel, the students, Beth Ann.

Beth Ann was happy for Vince, but adamant. "Vince, please try to understand what this means to me. We just can't leave. Not now. We have too much to do here.

"I know why you had to go down there. I am happy for you, and happy that you are happy. I know what it means to you to know that someone wants you. But can't you somehow accept that so that we can go on with our lives here in Wheatheart?"

"It is not over, Beth Ann. Don't you understand? This is just the beginning."

"We don't have beginnings anymore. We are too old for that. There has been too much water under the bridge. We are what we are, Vince. Maybe we made ourselves this way, but it doesn't matter how we got here. This is now the way we are."

"But I am not satisfied with that. Why does it have to be that way?"

"Because we have roots. We have stayed here too long and we have grown roots. Deep roots." She meant it.

"What kind of roots? This house, those sporty cars, a boat we never use?"

"You know better than that. Those are things, not roots. Sure, I like to have nice things. Maybe that is why I am willing to work so hard. But I don't *have* to have them."

"Then what are the roots?"

"Things like dependability and responsibility and what people expect from us. We've grown roots into the lives of a lot of people. We can't leave all that."

"Well, I don't know about you, but I don't need those roots. Not anymore. I proved that at Corpus yesterday. I thought maybe I needed this place like some kind of security blanket, that outside of here I would fall on my face. But I didn't. I taught that class and I taught them as well as anybody could. I knew that just by looking at them. I don't need these roots."

"Maybe these roots need you."

"Beth Ann." He paused and called up his best courtroom cross-examination tone. "Why are you afraid to leave?"

"Why are you afraid to stay?"

Vince was not surprised that the breakfast crowd at the Dew Drop Inn had already heard about his trip to Corpus Christi and the yet unsigned contract in his pocket. News, real news, travels fast in Wheatheart, and this was real news. Deaths, births, accidents, hospitalizations, engagements, and football scores were all news. When there weren't any things like that to report, the midwinter conversations dealt with the regular topics of wheat prices, moisture, old stories, and the health of the young plants, particularly their roots.

The comings and goings and other human antics of school people, particularly coaches and principals, were lead features. Such people belonged to the community. To earn the trust they needed to function for the community, they gave up their right to private lives. It was bigger than being trusted with the children or even education. School activities assumed chamber of commerce roles, and all school people became public relations figures.

If Vince resigned, it would be more than a Wheatheart issue. This kind of news would spread all over the area, all over the western part of the state; other towns which hated Wheatheart for its athletic success would ask in tones reserved for scandal, "I wonder what is *really* going on down there."

Vince was not surprised to find that he had already made the news. And he wasn't all that surprised at the community's collective response.

When he walked in, he heard the forced hush, like the hush in the boys' restroom when he walks in unexpectedly and is serenaded with a sudden flush of toilets. After twenty-three years in the school, nine as a principal, Vince learned to sense when he had stopped a conversation in which he was the main topic.

After some deliberate attempts to start a new discussion on the mundane and regular topics failed, the conversation came around to Vince and his problem. He knew it would and they knew it would. Both parties were just trying to be nice in the delay, trying to keep within the boundaries of acceptable Dew Drop Inn etiquette.

"So, Vince, you got a wild idea to run off to Texas?"

"It's the big city, I hear." And the group broke out into laughter. It was an uneasy, unreal laughter, but both Vince and his conversation adversaries were grateful, because it eased the tension.

"Well, I just went down to look around." Vince tried to be as casual as he could. He was still the principal, and this was an official school report. But the comments came from all over the room. Though each of the speakers thought he was being persuasively creative, they all said the same things, over and over again.

"Don't know why you want to leave with everything you've got here."

"Well, just look at this year alone. State football team. Don't that mean nothing?"

"You've got the best house in town and your wife's got the best job." No one mentioned her current problems.

"How much better can you have than that?"

"You won't see kids like ours down there, I'll tell you that."

"If you ask me, I would stay away from that place. You get down there with all those dopers and you get problems you can't handle."

"You've been here too long to pull up your roots now."

"I'm glad it's you that wants to go instead of me." In the minds of the patriotic Wheatheart people, drugs and crime ran rampant in any city or village more than fifty miles away.

Vince wanted to shout. He wanted to tell them he had taught in Corpus Christi and had taught well. Life was bigger than drugs and fights in halls and keeping a lid on things. He was an English teacher—a good one. But they couldn't understand that, not these people who got their thrills out of nice rains and football victories.

But then the friendly persuasion wore thin and the comments turned almost nasty. "I wonder what the school board is going to say about this. You know, if I was on that board, I wouldn't let you leave. I heard about that happening out in the Yukon or somewhere. Just wouldn't let the guy go."

Again, Vince wanted to stay and defend himself, but it was late and he had to get to school. As he was leaving, he heard Moss Bosco adding his part to the morning proceedings. "That sure is a pretty place down there with all those palm trees. They don't grow native you know, like our trees around here, helter-skelter. No, sir, they are all planted. You have better lines that way. More order."

The school day, up until the first period lull, was closer to normal than Vince had thought it would be. He had expectations, and those did color comments and events which on other days would have been mere routine. He policed the halls, greeted the teachers, listened to excuses, wrote admits, and announced a lost book on the intercom. Miss Helen McClurg greeted the news with a sneer and a snide remark, "I don't see how we can expect these kids to have any sense of responsibility when the adults around here don't show any." But since this was usual for her, he didn't let either the look or the comment bother him. And he managed to make it into his office and close the door at the beginning of the lull.

Maybe this wasn't going to be as bad a day as he thought. But just about the time he was going to relax with his thoughts and perhaps the last pages of *Portrait of an Artist as a Young Man,* which he had boldly moved up to his office from the basement hiding place a few days before the New Orleans trip, a gentle rap on the door disturbed him back into more immediate demands, and two cheerleaders walked in. They were carrying a cake, beautifully decorated with white icing heaped with coconut.

"Mr. Benalli," the senior cheerleader captain spoke. This was her right of office. Being a spokesperson earned her the office in the first place.

"Yes." He was a bit stunned and embarrassed about what he thought was going to happen.

"We have a present for you. The cheerleaders. We want you to have this."

He acted pleased and shocked. "Why, what's the occasion?"

They both looked pleasantly impatient, as if to say, "Let's not play games. We all know why we are here." But they didn't mention it. Instead, the junior said, "We just wanted to do something nice for a nice person, and you are about the nicest person we know. So here it is—we hope you enjoy it."

"Thank you." Vince wanted to say more. The girls wanted to say more. But more had already been said than was spoken, so Vince decided to let the communication take root in silence. The three of them stood and looked at each other for a brief but profound moment, and then the girls walked out.

As Vince was putting the cake up on top of the filing cabinet so he could enjoy it during the day, both as a real thing and as a symbol, Miss Helen McClurg stuck her head in the door and yelled. "You had better come quick. We've got trouble."

Vince knew that tone well enough not to make light of it or even to find fault. He rushed out behind her, turned into what should have been the lull-filled hall and ran into a small group of students gathered around two wild animals wrestling on the floor with the intensity of sincere malice. He slipped through the crowd and pulled the two beasts apart. With his short but stout arms, Vince managed to hold them apart long enough to identify the people, Bobby Golden and Craig Brady, and to assess the damage. Both were disheveled and bruised and scratched.

Without saying a word, Vince drew himself up to his full principal's stature and literally dragged the pugilists through the hall and into his office where he threw each into a chair on opposite sides of the room. For minutes he stood and stared at them, trying to regain his own breath and his own control—until he decided not to war against his feelings.

"Both of you. Get on that phone and call your mothers to come get you. You are out of here. In three days, come back in to see me with your parents. We aren't going to have this. Not in this school. Now call. I don't want to see you around here."

"Don't you want to hear my side?" Craig asked, trying to sound as innocent as he could.

"You don't have a side." Vince raised his voice as he spoke. "Not anymore. Neither of you." And he tried to analyze why he was so angry. He wasn't this angry when they fought before, but maybe that is what bothered him. That whole winter had come and gone and they hadn't learned a thing. By fighting again, they had actually betrayed Vince. After the last scuffle, he had gone all over town defending them—telling everybody that they were good friends. Now they fought again, as if to prove that Vince didn't know what he was talking about—that he really didn't know these kids after all. The three of them sat in silence until the mothers came and took the boys home. Of course, Vince would have to attend to the nuisance details of the incident—writing letters explaining his action and telling the parents how to appeal his decision. That was bad enough, but the hurt would linger on, even after he had forgotten this whole day and the cause.

Before he had time to collect his thoughts or feel sorry for himself or begin his chores, two loud raps jarred the door and Casteel came raging in like an angry wave. Vince wasn't ready for this, not just yet, but Casteel was sometimes hard to take even when one was prepared, so he chose to make the best of it.

"What's this I hear?" Casteel frequently used this approach to open conversations. Vince diagnosed it as a form of subconscious manipulation. Since he didn't know what Casteel had heard already, he had to guess and that guessing put him on the defensive. Casteel had scored the first point of their mental battle with an ambiguous question. But maybe Vince could play the game too.

"Well, if you heard it, I guess it must be true."

"The board is not going to like it. I can tell you that. After everything we have done for you, seems like you would have more loyalty than that. I'll tell you one thing, if this is just a plot to ask us for more money, it isn't going to work."

Vince was relieved to ascertain the nature of the conversation, but he was angry with the accusation. Yes, angry. Vince hadn't been really angry in months, maybe years. He might have been tired and bored and even disillusioned and impatient. But not angry. How can you be angry with people you feel sorry for? The two emotions don't go together. But today Vince was angry. That fight in the hall had stirred him up. Maybe in the excitement he had let himself escape into anger as a form of protection against other emotions battling for his feelings; but whatever the reason, he was angry and it showed.

For the first time in all his years of listening to Casteel talk, he took the lead. "Let me tell you something. This isn't an attempt to get money. I don't owe this school anything and this school doesn't owe me anything. I am a good teacher, a good school man, and I plan to put that to use for people who will appreciate me." He stopped to get his breath, and Casteel interrupted him matter-of-factly.

"We know you are a good school man. That's why you ought to stay here. We already know what you can do. You don't have to prove anything." With that, Casteel turned and walked out with the same air of undaunted confidence he had walked in with.

Through a sense of duty, Vince found enough mental stability that morning to perform his chores. He stayed in his office, though, with the door shut, through the passing times, through the lounge breaks. He wrote the requisite letters, charted attendance figures, and in general, executed the paperwork which went with the office of principal. But all this was delay and he knew it. An unmade decision is the most relentless of dictators, and Vince couldn't go through the rest of the day, much less the rest of the year, shut away in his office. He had to take the issue in hand.

But why was it so hard? He was an administrator, a manager, trained in the art of decision-making. He made decisions every day, hundreds of them, and sometimes those decisions were serious and significant, decisions which could determine a young person's development and destiny. Whose name do I submit for this honor? What do I say on that recommendation? Do I kick them out of school for three days for fighting in the hall? He managed to make those decisions every day without all this agony. Maybe it's different, easier, to make decisions which affect others and not yourself. Somewhere down the road you eventually became the victim of your own previous decisions. Vince knew that, and because he knew that, he suffered.

Yet there had to be a less painful way to go about this. He would just apply the system. It had worked before when he had to choose which teacher to hire from several applicants, or when he had to select textbooks in areas he didn't know well, or when he planned cheerleader tryout ceremonies. The system was a good one. It provided objective perspective.

So he reached into his desk and pulled out a new legal pad. The more important decisions demand new legal pads. He took his straightedge and drew a vertical line dividing the top sheet into two columns. At the top of the left-hand column he wrote, Reasons To Stay. At the top of the right-hand column he wrote Reasons To Go. In the left-hand column the first items on the list came easily, and he wrote without the need to doodle along the edges.

Beth Ann's job
Our house

> My salary
> The cake (as a symbol)
> Community prestige
> Roots

Now the list got harder, and he worked more slowly pondering each item amidst several attempts in between to create a balanced diagram of assorted lines and shapes at the edge of the paper.

> Success
> Acceptance
> Breakfast at the Dew Drop Inn

He smiled as he wrote the last one. How he hated that place, and how he loved it. After a long time, after he had chewed the pen cap into an unrecognizable form and had completed his marginal art work, he wrote his one final entry.

> Rose

Now that the left side was finished, he needed to develop his list on the right to balance it out and even things up. This time he sat quietly, no doodling and no pen chewing, and he remembered his walk on the seawall along the bay, and he remembered his interview, and he remembered and remembered with vivid recall himself in front of that class. But he didn't write anything. He just stared at that empty column which looked so neat and orderly and lonely. And finally, with the pen resting in his hand, he bent down and scribbled in that right-hand column.

46

He crumpled the sheet of paper and threw it toward the wastebasket. As it rebounded off the side of the desk and fell into the wargreen receptacle, the whole situation reminded him of a scene from his youth when basketballs fell frequently through rims. And that vision of a basketball going through a rim was always a pleasant one. Fulfilled basketball goals are the rewards of hard work and order, of a timed and coordinated move in the midst of chaos. Remembering this, Vince had a strong impulse to shoot a basketball again. Knowing the gym would be empty this period, he decided it would be good to add some physical movement to his reflection. So as quietly as he could, he left his office and headed toward the gym. Fortunately, the halls were empty at this time of day. Vince hadn't seen any students since early morning, before he had suspended the two boys, and he didn't know how that news would affect the school. He knew what it would do for the town. By now every gossipmonger within miles was making the most of the day's bounty: Benalli has an offer to leave. Craig and Bobby were fighting in the hall. The boys have been suspended! There hadn't been this much news in Wheatheart since the explosion at the co-op elevator last fall. Vince was providing the town a little excitement, and he didn't want to face anybody for a follow-up discussion.

And he almost made it too until one of the cheerleaders, the senior captain, came out of the English room. She could do that. She was a school leader, and going to class was only secondary in her educational priorities. She had just been excused from class to handle some matter more important than reading *Macbeth*. When she saw Vince, she smiled pleasantly, even appreciatively, and said, "We hope you enjoy your cake, Mr. Benalli."

He was happy for the comment. He was also happy to find a basketball lying in the corner of the gym, just waiting to perform its created mission, to fly high above the rim and fall through in the exact middle, making the net below fill the gym with that pleasant sound of "whoosh," which, being interpreted, means, "The ball is in the hoop and all's right with the world."

Vince kicked off his shoes, picked up the ball, and tried the famous Benalli corner special. But just as he brought the ball up for proper sighting, his back creaked, the muscles hardened from the unusual move, and his legs acutely protested his command to jump.

Without all body parts in working order, he missed the shot by nearly ten feet. But Vince wasn't dismayed. He had time. So he shot and he shot and he shot. He hit a few things, attempts in close, the flips and some nonjump layups. But he never hit a longer shot, one of the old-time jumps which had made him famous as a player and a young coach scrimmaging against his players. The rhythm which had made him all-conference was gone, and shooting baskets wasn't fun anymore.

But Vince didn't want to go back into the building. Not now. He just wasn't ready. He didn't want to see the people. He just wanted to be alone in an environment which would accommodate and respond to his mood.

Then he thought of Wagner's Pond. The last time he had been in a strange mood, Wagner's Pond had helped. He might as well try it today—he wasn't doing the school any good anyway.

He checked his coat pocket to make sure he had a pen and a good writing tablet with lots of blank pages. Then he got into his sporty car and drove away.

19

Struggling for Life
1981

The day was cold and brilliantly clear. It had been unusually cold for the past few weeks, even for February, and it seemed particularly cold now, since Vince had just been to Corpus Christi on the bay.

As he drove over the hill overlooking Wagner's Pond, he was struck by the reflection. A prism of light, sent forth by the sun, the symbol of warmth, rebounded off the ice which froze the pond into perfect stillness. It wasn't the same as the last time he had seen it under the November moonlight, but it was all quiet and beautiful in a new sort of way. Vince tried to remember when he had seen Wagner's Pond look like this.

He drove up to the edge of the pond and stepped out of his car. The sound of shouting from the water disturbed the silence and pushed Vince—for the first time today—out of his introspection and into service. He soon placed the shouts in the middle of the pond, as he saw one form—no, two forms—flailing helplessly in the cold water. He recognized the forms—he had seen them before, flailing just as helplessly—Bobby Golden and Craig Brady.

In a quick assessment of the visible evidences, Vince knew the whole story. The shotguns lying carelessly on the bank told him that the boys had decided to use their suspension time for bird hunting. Somebody had shot a bird which had fallen on the ice. The boy went after it. The ice broke and he fell into the freezing water. The other boy, in a spirit of dutiful heroism, went out to retrieve his friend. And now they were both trapped in the middle of the pond, unable to get out because of the heavy boots and clothes which weighted them down.

Vince couldn't tell how long they had been in the water, but they were already past the state of coherence. Irrationally, they beat at the water, struggling to keep their heads above, to hold onto the only thing that really mattered—the fragment of life they still had left. They yelled frantically, impulsively, crying out for rescue from the consequence of their own poor judgment.

Vince realized that he didn't have much time. They had been in the water too long already and were in danger from both drowning and freezing to death. It was just a matter of which came first. But Vince also knew that he needed help. Even if he managed to get them ashore, he would need a vehicle to take them into the hospital before illness or cold destroyed them. But if he went for help, he would be too late to pull them out. So he decided to risk his chance at doing both. He drove his car, his sporty new Firebird, as near to the water's edge as he dared. With instinct trained by years of judgment, he rummaged through his stereo tapes until he found the right one, Beethoven's final movement of the *Gloria* from the *Missi Solemnis*. He then turned the "loudest stereo he had ever heard" on full blast. With that, he started taking off his own clothes, as far as he could tolerate—jacket, pants, shirt—and tied sleeves and legs together making a cloth chain. But it wasn't long enough. He had to have more . . . Then he remembered an ancient costume, hidden away in a remote corner of his car, hidden away like forgotten garbage. Vince pulled out a blue silk shirt with white flecks and designer jeans, size 38, and added those pieces to his chain.

He tied the chain to the bumper of his car and gradually, clinging to the homemade rope, let himself across the pond. When the ice broke and dropped him into the freezing water, he lost his breath and consciousness momentarily and he had to remind himself to breathe. When he recovered, he felt the pain, excruciating pain. Not muscle cramps . . . worse than that . . . the pain of cold water working against warm skin, robbing it of the body heat it still had left. Cold, vicious water punished him for penetrating its serenity. But by now he was close to the boys, close enough to grab one and carry out some of his mission. Which boy wasn't important. He grabbed at random and got Craig, which was just as well. Although both were in a state of unconscious frantic, Craig was more subdued than Bobby who was struggling at his maximum just to keep afloat. Though he was a first team back in state championship football, he probably didn't know how to swim.

With Vince's pull, Craig glided easily through the water and together they worked themselves back to the clothes chain. Craig grabbed the dangling sleeve of an expensive silk shirt and had enough life left in him to remember to pull himself, by his own strength, back to the bank and temporary safety.

Getting Bobby was harder. Bobby fought against Vince's attempt to bring him to the edge of the ice, and the ensuing wrestle pulled them both underneath. With the added weight of Bobby's wet winter clothes, it was all Vince could do to lift them both back so their heads could break the surface of the water. Vince was too exhausted for the struggle and he knew he had to take quick action. Any more of this and they both would be on the bottom of the pond. So he did the only thing he could think of—he slapped Bobby as hard as he could. In the midst of danger, he thought to himself, "I have been wanting to do that all day." He was chuckling, actually chuckling, when he pulled Bobby through the water to the clothes rope, and climbed the rope to the bank with Bobby lying quietly under his arm.

As he came out of the water, the cold air brought another chilling shock to his body, and now they had to find some way to stay warm enough to live until someone came. Perhaps they could take the car, but Vince was too tired and too disoriented to make the car work. They had to depend on help coming. The car stereo blared loud and the genius of Beethoven's finest filled the prairie. Vince picked up the two boys, as if they were sacks of lifeless wheat seed, threw them on top of each other, and jumped on top of the pile himself. "If any of us has any body heat left, we may as well share it," Vince thought. Now his biggest job was to keep awake, to stay alert so his body temperature would not decrease with sleep. He worked at fighting back the fatigue and the pain and the heaviness, but he couldn't win. Even the blaring sounds of the stereo seemed melodious and soothing. Vince surrendered to the impulse and fell asleep.

20

Reaching Beyond the Man
1981

Vince awoke into a hazy reality. He slowly recognized the distinctive features of a hospital room—the sterile look combined with the medical odor. He saw Beth Ann beside his bed, smiling encouragingly. He tried to turn over but found his body movement restricted by tubes and soreness. He made a halfhearted effort at shaking the confusion of sleep from his mind, but it was too much work, so he gave up and dozed off again.

He repeated this whole operation several times, always coming back around to Beth Ann sitting close by, until finally, he gained the strength it took to fight back sleep and gather his thoughts and memories. It all came back in irregular episodes arranged in almost chronological order so he was able to piece it together and catch himself up to the present. Encouraged by Beth Ann's presence, he spoke, almost surprising himself with the sound of his voice and with the words which flowed out of his automatic speech mechanism. "How long have I been asleep?"

Her smile was part of a standard hospital manner designed to reassure, but it was more than that. It was a symbol of a deeper joy, almost like the look she had years ago, after Vince's team would win a crucial game. "Almost two days now."

"Two days?" His voice and inflection were weak but his desire to know was strong. "Am I sick?"

She was helpful. "You've got a couple of little problems. You were awfully cold when they brought you in, so they had to warm you up first. And now you've got a touch of pneumonia. But Doc Heimer says you are going to be just fine. You just slept a long time as a way of gaining your strength back."

A frightening image worked itself across his mind, and he asked, "What about the boys?"

"They're fine, both of them. They were cold too. But they're younger and maybe a little tougher than you, so they have recovered faster. They have been asking about you."

By now, it was important to Vince to have the whole plot laid out in front of him, so he was eager to fill in the gaps. "How did we get here?"

There was almost laughter in her voice as she answered. "George Wagner heard your car stereo, playing Beethoven of all things. He called Earl Bresserman and they all got there about the same time. You were still wet, so you must not have been out of the water very long." She went on. "You're a real hero, Vince. You made the *Daily Oklahoman,* front page even. Let me read it to you. See—it's set in boxes like a major news story, all right, but with a happy ending." She read:

Vince Benalli, principal of Wheatheart High School, rescued a couple of his students Wednesday afternoon the hard way. Benalli, a popular teacher at the school and former basketball coach before he became principal, found two of his students, Craig Brady and Bobby Golden, both members of the Class A State championship football team, after they had fallen through the ice at a nearby farm pond. The boys had apparently gone to the pond to hunt quail.

163

Benalli pulled both students out of the icy water before Earl Bresserman, town sheriff, and several area farmers arrived to help. Bresserman credited Benalli's quick thinking and daring action for saving the two young hunters. "He not only signaled for help but he made a rope out of old clothes so he wouldn't have to drag them so far."

George Wagner, a local farmer and owner of the pond, commented on how he was alerted to the danger. "I heard this car stereo playing real loud. It was playing some of that classical, long-haired stuff, and I knew the only guy in town who played that was Benalli, and I knew he wouldn't play it that loud unless he was in trouble. So I called for help and went to check." He added, "If it had been any other kind of music, I probably wouldn't have thought much about it, just a bunch of kids playing their radio loud, but not that long-haired stuff."

Benalli and the boys are in stable condition in the Wheatheart Hospital.

As she finished reading, Beth Ann added her own commentary. "See, I've got a real hero on my hands."

Vince lay staring at the tubes running in and out of his body as he tried to identify with the person in that article, but he had trouble making a flesh-and-blood connection.

"You say I have been here two days?"

"Yes."

"But you were here every time I woke up."

She answered so gently but firmly. "You're all I've got, Vince. You're not just the most important. You're the only one who matters. I had to be here."

He liked the answer. It wasn't something she had to say because he was sick or even because he was a hero. She said it because it was true. So for minutes and perhaps hours, he lay and she sat, the two of them, being quiet together.

Finally, just before she needed to go home for a while, in a very casual manner, she tested the renewed health of their relationship. "Vince, there is a question everybody in town is dying to ask; but if I know this town, nobody ever will. But you had better prepare for it just in case."

"Yes?" Vince drew out the word as long as he could, trying to anticipate and prepare himself for the weight of something shocking.

"Why were you out there at Wagner's Pond that time of day in the first place?" There, she had asked it. Everybody else was thinking it, but no one else would ask. But she had asked. She was his wife and she had a right to ask. She had a right to know motives and reasons.

Vince could muster only the structure of an answer. "I had to think." That was enough; she understood. And she left pleasantly and cheerfully, as if to say the issue would never come up again.

Over the next few days, a steady stream of Wheatheart society poured through Vince's room. Young and old, the successful and the small-time borrowers, close friends and distant, the powerful and the cautious—they all came, probably for different reasons, but they brought warmth, appreciation, curiosity, and tokens of their caring.

Bobby and Craig came as soon as the nurse told them Vince was awake enough to talk. They kidded him about his physical shape for an old man, and reported on their state of health. Each was doing well, except that Bobby had a bad bruise on the side of his face—probably scraped it against the ice. At least, that's what Doc thought. Vince measured the courage it would take to correct a community rumor, particularly a popular one heavily steeped in the credibility of public opinion, and decided not to bother.

Although the boys never said, "Thanks," not in adult words at least, they communicated with adolescent sincerity in a structure which wouldn't embarrass anyone. Since Vince was experienced in talking with adolescents, he recognized the unspoken thoughts and accepted them.

But just in case Vince was still in doubt about how these two young men felt about him, how they felt about each other, how they felt about life itself, there was one more reminder. As they were leaving his room to wander on back down the hall to cheer up other patients and to celebrate in general, Craig stopped at the door, leaned back partially into the room as if he were partly serious but mostly teasing, and asked, "By the way, Mr. Benalli, do these three days in the hospital count against our suspension time?" His wide grin, just short of a laugh, put that whole issue in perspective, and he ambled on down the hall, leaving Vince with his thoughts to prepare for more company.

Art and Scott Garland stopped to visit, but Vince couldn't tell whether they came as mayor, as merchants, or as friends. It didn't really matter. They were pleasant even though they did seem officious.

The cheerleaders dropped in, en masse, all six of them, giggling and chewing gum, since they were out of school. Together they had carved out of poster board a large Whippet, and every student in school had signed it with green magic marker, every student except the two freshmen who were out with chicken pox.

Rosemary from the cafe couldn't come, but she cooked a cheeseburger, just the way Vince liked it, and sent it up to the hospital with Moss Bosco who brought Vince an original painting. It was a seascape which Moss had copied from an art book he had bought down in the City several years ago.

Charlie Brady came especially to express his gratitude to Vince for risking his own neck to save his grandson. Charlie was so appreciative that he stayed for nearly three hours and entertained Vince with stories and legends about Wheatheart and its people. Although Vince had heard most of the stories before, he acted as if he hadn't, because Charlie had a need to make him feel better.

Earl Bresserman came on official police business. He wanted to recommend that the town council give Vince some kind of special recognition for his act of valor. Such actions on the parts of citizens were important to community security, and Vince deserved to be recognized. It would help the whole community, but Earl wanted to get Vince's permission first. Then Earl remembered another official matter.

"Vince," he asked just before he left. "What do you want us to do with your clothes that we pulled out of the pond? They're pretty wet and rotten right now, but we still have them, if you want them back."

A trace of a smile worked itself across Vince's mouth as he remembered those clothes, not his own clothes which he had shed for the rope, but that costume he had stashed away in the back of his car so long ago when he was in a different stage of his life. But he couldn't dwell on such thoughts with an official policeman in the room, so he remembered the other garments. "No. I don't think I want any of that stuff, but go through the pockets before you destroy anything."

"Oh, we did that." Earl acted as if his competence had been challenged.

"What did you find?" Vince disarmed him with a sincere question.

"Just the usual, some change, a small pocketknife, your money clip. And you know, those bills weathered that water in good shape. Still spendable."

"Is that all?"

"Yeah, I think so. We searched everything pretty thoroughly. Why?"

"Oh, I had some important papers in my jacket pocket."

"They weren't there. We would have found them if they had been there. I'm sorry."

"Oh, it isn't anything. I can get duplicates if I decide I need them."

"Sorry." Earl said that like he meant it. Here this citizen had risked his life to save somebody and he lost his important papers.

Vince reassured him. "Forget it. It wasn't all that important." And with that, Earl went back to policing the streets of Wheatheart.

Mr. Casteel came. He really wanted to tell Vince that he had missed him, that he was proud of him for being so brave, that he hoped he recovered soon and completely. That is what Casteel really wanted to say, or at least that is what Vince felt he wanted to say. But he didn't say any of those things. He entered abruptly, conducted business, and left just as abruptly. But he did ask for Vince's opinion on several school problems, and he acted as if that opinion mattered. And from this, Vince read warmth and cordiality and care into the visit.

When Brother Bob made his customary hospital rounds, he found Vince in a contemplative mood. In fact, Vince had chosen to use some of this time to try to remember that short series of sermons on the seeds of faith. And he was glad to see the preacher because they could remember together. But Brother Bob had forgotten just what he had said. Oh, he made a polite attempt to remember, but those sermons were something he had performed months ago, and the ideas were no longer clear in his mind.

Between visits from the rest of the community, Beth Ann dropped in and out frequently, every time she could catch a few minutes to get away and run over. She was so pleasant and cheerful that Vince looked forward to those unexpected visits, and he got better each time she came. She caught him up on town gossip, not just the talk and the events but the news behind the news which nobody except his wife would dare share with him. She fluffed his pillow and tidied his room as only a wife could do. She brought the mail, and generally expressed her love and concern and pride in her hero husband.

During one of these visits, as they were deeply entrenched in the communication of silence that only husbands and wives of many years can understand, she broke the silence with her voice but probably didn't interrupt the thoughts of either.

"Vince." She studied the rest of her remark carefully before she made it. "We can go to Texas."

"What?" He had heard but he needed time to grasp what he had heard.

"I've resigned." She was matter-of-fact.

"Beth Ann!" he pleaded with her, almost admonishing her.

"It isn't what you think," she protested with a smile in her voice.

Vince still wasn't satisfied. He could only think of two reasons for her to quit—because of him or because of the board of directors, and he didn't like either reason. That would have meant that she had given in to somebody and he didn't want her to give in. But she reassured him by repeating herself, this time with almost a chuckle. "It isn't what you think."

Vince still didn't understand. "What happened?"

"I won!" She said it like she was the basketball coach with the first state championship in that sport in the history of Wheatheart.

"You won?" He thought he knew what she meant, but he wasn't sure.

"Last week over in Blaine County two of those drilling companies filed bankruptcy petitions. I don't know why I am happy about that. It is really sad. Those drillers are going to leave town owing people thousands of dollars—money which they will never collect. They bought all that expensive equipment and did all that work just to accumulate a lot of bad debts. Of course, it is different on those wells which hit; but on the dry holes, someone has to stand the expense. Right now it looks like it is going to be the subcontractors, struggling people who just saw an opportunity to get rich quick. And now they're going to lose everything. And eventually, the banks are going to get hit too. They have got to repossess, and they can't sell the equipment, not for what they lent on it. This is a bad deal, Vince. It is going to affect a lot of banks, even big ones in Oklahoma City and maybe even in places like Chicago."

Vince lay in silence as she related the whole story. He didn't interrupt her or interject little phrases to stir her on. He didn't have to. She was excited to tell the story, as if she needed to keep all the details clear. "So you won?"

"Vince, I was right all along. Now I know why."

As he contemplated the information, a happy image came to his mind. "Does your board know?"

She laughed. "You'll never believe it. Mr. Oscar Pritchett, Jr. sent me flowers."

"Flowers?" Vince was laughing but he was still shocked. That image was too strange for Oscar Pritchett.

Beth Ann was still a little shocked too. "A dozen long-stemmed roses. Mattie delivered them to the bank."

Both of them laughed as they enjoyed the twist and each other. Vince asked, "What did the card say?"

Tears came to Beth Ann's eyes as she choked herself with laughter and mustered an answer. "It was sentimental. It said, 'Oscar Pritchett, Jr. and the Board of Directors.' "

As the laughter subsided with diminishing outbursts, Vince turned philosophical with a rhetorical question bigger than Oscar Pritchett and the bank board and Wheatheart High School. "I wonder why it's so hard for people to say, 'I'm sorry.' "

Since Beth Ann had been thinking the same thing and couldn't find an answer, she only added, "It would be a lot cheaper," and both of them laughed again.

But then Vince remembered the origin of the conversation. "But you said you resigned?"

A pleasant seriousness came back to her eyes. "I sure did, Vince. After it was all over and those flowers came, I sat there at my desk and asked myself what I could be doing if I wasn't doing this. And I liked the answers I came up with. The bank is in good shape. We don't need my salary anymore and we could even get by without some of our things. It isn't like I am running away. After all, when I took this job, we both agreed that it was only temporary." And they chuckled again, partly because they were in this mood and partly because both of them remembered that conversation years ago.

But now it was Vince's time to ponder. "Beth Ann?"

"Yes." She reassured him again.

"What if I decide I don't want that position in Texas?"

She was calm and sincerely reassuring. "It's up to you, whatever you want. You're my husband. You do what is best for us.''

"But what would you do?'' Vince had trouble imagining Beth Ann outside the bank, and he had to ask.

Her mouth formed a strange expression, somewhere between a light smile and an object of wisdom. "I am going to be your wife. I don't need anything else.''

Vince rolled that insight through his now fertile mind, hoping he could give the idea enough nourishment so that it could flower. He liked the wisdom and security. For the first time in a long time, he knew what she meant, and he did not need to press for more.

He still had a decision to make himself. That number-one item he had put on his decision list several days ago had just gone away. Beth Ann's job wasn't a cause anymore. So now he had to look at this list again, but through a different set of eyes.

Mostly he was the same person who had gone to Corpus Christi, who had gone to New Orleans. He was the same person who kicked those boys out of school and dived into Wagner's Pond. He was the same person—still Vince Benalli and still forty-six. But he was different. Beth Ann was different. And they were different together.

Maybe recent events helped bring that difference—Beth Ann's status at the bank and his alleged heroism—but those events weren't really causes. They were only ripples leading out to the causes, whatever they were.

Vince and Beth Ann were so comfortable together, even in silence, that he missed her when she had to leave for a few hours.

Coach Rose came, and out of all the visitors, except for Beth Ann, he was the most casual and the most comfortable. He came in, sat on the edge of the bed, helped Vince adjust the pillows, asked what he could do, and told Vince the little personal stories designed to document his point that the school was slightly out of tilt while Vince was away. There were no major problems, but the routine just didn't flow. And Vince listened to his best friend and felt warm inside and out.

And then, rather deliberately, Rose took a more serious tone, as if something had been bothering him.

"Vincent, years ago we had a discussion. You've probably forgotten it, long gone. But it was important to me and I still think about it once in awhile."

Vince was eager but still a bit cautious about where this might lead. "What about?"

"One night at a coaching clinic, you asked me what courage was."

"I remember," Vince added quickly. He wanted to assure Coach Rose that he was not in this conversation alone.

"Well, I don't know what I told you then. Some youthful idealism probably. You know, I used to have a lot more answers than I have now. It all used to be a lot simpler. Have you noticed the older you get the harder it gets to define words you used to know the definition of? Success—fifteen, twenty years ago, I used to tell these kids every day what success was, and now I don't even know myself anymore. Fulfillment. Hope. I am not really sure I know the meaning of any of those things anymore, Vincent. And courage? I don't know what that is. And you know what scares me? Some of these days, I am going to have to answer these questions, and I don't know how. Do you know what I mean?"

Vince's simple, "Yes," did not reveal all the agony and thoughts and frustrations heaped into it; but on the other hand, maybe it did.

Nevertheless, it was enough answer for Rose. He went on. "Okay. Now it's my turn. You've been there. What is courage?"

Vince answered as truthfully as he knew how. "I don't know. I still don't know. But it isn't what I did. That isn't courage. That's automatic. You don't even think about those things. You just react. And somehow when you are just living every day, you just know that if the time ever comes, that's the way you are going to react. At first, I was surprised with myself. But I am not anymore. I was in a trance all the time. There was nothing real or thought out about it. All automatic. So I still don't know what courage is."

Rose accepted his answer reluctantly. "I wish you did know. I wish you had found out. It would sure be a lot simpler."

Vince agreed. "Yeah, I know what you mean. According to all the people around here, this is the bravest thing I have ever done in my life and I had my eyes closed all the way through it." Their mutual laughter helped break the intensity which held them in its spell.

But Vince wasn't through. "Coach." In this context, the title was a term of respect, symbolically respectful. "One thing I did learn."

"What's that?" Both were back in a serious mood in an instant.

"It does make a difference."

"What?"

"It does make a difference." Vince waited for the question to follow so he could clear up this matter completely. But there was no question, and the look on Rose's face showed that he understood, that he too was glad to know the answer.

Vince read the reaction, but went on anyway. "When I saw those kids out there, struggling to live, I realized what we should have known all along. It makes a difference—you and I being here—what we do. It isn't an accident. It is all on purpose."

Again both men individually contemplated the implications of that last statement. Finally, Coach Rose, the winningest coach in Oklahoma football history, and the most respected and revered man in all of Wheatheart, observed, "Yeah, I know what you mean. When you quit hiding behind the nonsense, and all the hype and all the surface glory, there is something about it that makes you know that you were meant to be here all along." After that, neither man said anything. A few minutes later, Coach Rose got up and walked out of the security of that isolated hospital room, back into a world where he was almost a king.

That day's mail brought a letter. Jimmy Charles Ericson could not get away from the farm to come visit, so he sent a note. Written in penmanship that looked like it belonged to a sophomore football player, the note read:

When the God in us reaches beyond the man in us,
only then can we feel the heavens and know who we are, and why!
Romans 8:28

Vince read the words over and over again, slowly and rapidly, in a monotone and with feeling, and he was glad that he was in the room alone. He could let all of his feelings and all of his thoughts turn ripe within him and flush his face and tingle his fingers. He wished he had written those words; and that thought angered him—not the kind of anger which takes its revenge on somebody, but the kind of anger you have toward yourself when you realize your own limits. Yet he was also pleased. Jostled by a sixteen-year-old mind, he realized his own limits, and that thought pleased him to the point of making tears that got in the way of his reading the words again.

Vince had taught composition too long and too well not to know the value of a theme. Every good life, like every good paper, has a theme, and Jimmy Charles had just pointed this out to him. His search made sense!

On that thought, Vince laid the note on the bed, put his hands behind his head, and rested. He glanced around his small, almost sterile looking room and remembered all the people who had visited him in the past few days. The room looked like Wheatheart, smelled like Wheatheart, and sounded like Wheatheart. And he said to himself silently, but aloud in his soul, "This is the stuff of pleasure." Suddenly, he found himself in touch with that mysterious yet knowable God who had brought him there and had put the stars in the sky and the students in school. And he never thought again, well, hardly ever, of that Corpus Christi contract which lay at the bottom of Wagner's Pond. And never again did he ask, "What difference does it make?"

Remember your Creator . . .
before the silver cord is severed,
or the golden bowl is broken;
before the pitcher is shattered at the spring,
or the wheel broken at the well,
and the dust returns to the ground it came from,
and the spirit returns to God who gave it.

Ecclesiastes 12:1, 6-7